# Daughters Lost to the Underworld

Daughters Lost to the Underworld

# DAUGHTERS LOST TO THE UNDERWORLD

Margaret Nyhon

# Contents

'To have been lost and found, these girls had journeys profound.'

'Drugs are counterfeit freedom, not to be confused with real freedom — there is no comparison.'

# Author's note

Links to my own personal experience in Australia, in resort management, form the basis of my novel.

True story: a drug syndicate operated out of one of our apartments and disguised themselves behind the good name of the Salvation Army. Stacks of money was seen through a window on many occasions. A young girl who was impaired by drugs left the resort at nights and walked down to the beach with a backpack. In the end, out of fear, we asked for police intervention, so their apartment was bugged.

To watch a person who is a drug addict is like watching a living person slowly dying while still alive. To be by their side while they recover is the most helpless situation: you can do nothing, but just to be there for them, always telling them they are loved. This can go on for however long ... their helplessness becomes your helplessness, but in the end, you are their guiding light, you must stay strong.

Into a scary lonely darkness they have descended, and while there, they have two choices: either stay in that darkness or claw their way back to where there is light. It is a battle of heroic proportions; one has to fight hard to rid harmful toxins from their body and demons from their mind, to find their palate to recover their appetite so they can hold food in their belly, to build themselves up again and, just as important, to find their lost soul!

I have travelled down this path with a loved one and shed rivers of tears, but I never gave up. In the end we survived this journey together. His pain was my pain, and shared it became one.

Facts became realistic fiction, hence my story. But out of this comes truths and fear. Should we be concerned? The answer is ... yes!

Illicit drugs are evil ... They steal away everything relating to normality, and robs one of the will to live, instead to become one who merely exists! Even when an addict recovers, their future aspirations have all but gone and they tend to live one day at a time.

# 1

# Lauren's life change

Lauren was standing by the window looking out to sea. The waves reminded her of her own turbulent life, as they rolled and crashed onto the rock groin, throwing spray angrily into the air. She was one of those particles that had been tossed about, but she had been rescued by a passing breeze that carried her to a new destination, one where she felt free. Her past was just that … her past.

Here she stood in this beautiful apartment block. She was now the proud owner, she had bought the management rights. This had been her life for the past ten years, not here, but elsewhere … this was a new beginning. The building housed seventeen apartments, some lived in full-time, some semi-permanent and the others were used as overnight rentals. It was a good mix and seventeen was a good amount for one person to manage. She was pleased with herself, she made this investment on her own without help, she didn't need Scott in the background needling her.

The apartments were in a half circle all facing the ocean,

beachfront in fact, and the view was to die for. A path led to a set of ten steps which in turn led to the beach. It was the pathway for the guests to reach the sand and surf, typical of a beachfront location on the Gold Coast. Who would want to stay anywhere else but on the beachfront when visiting or staying in such a popular destination? It was a must. Although situated on the outskirts of the main shopping precinct of Surfers Paradise, it was a little less stressful than right in the main drag. A bus service passed every ten minutes so transportation was not a problem, the ocean and the beaches being the main drawcards.

Lauren loved the views from her apartment, she felt relaxed. The building was only two years old, so the upkeep would be minimal. She sighed, at last she was a free agent, and this in itself made her happy. She felt she had found her lost soul, which had been missing for a long time. After living with Scott for the past ten years, she felt drained of all her self-worth. He had taken over her life, controlled her, she was his puppet and he held the strings. How had it all come to this?

But here she was today, a new person, with a positive attitude to succeed on her own. She thought it would have taken her a long time to find herself, but the moment her ties with Scott were severed, she had bounced back far sooner than she could have imagined. The suffocation had ended. As she took a deep breath and inhaled the sea air, it was as if all the stale air that had lingered and impeded her thinking had vanished. Now a fresh new mind was emerging from the upheaval of the past. She had backed herself when applying to buy the management rights and she had come out on top. Lauren never believed in miracles, but they did happen — she had just experienced one!

Her belongings were arriving later in the day in a north-bound furniture carrier, not that there was much, as her apartment was fully furnished. She did have a few personal treasures that couldn't be left behind, they were part of her life. There had been some good times earlier in the piece, but these had quickly faded. She slid open the glass sliding doors and walked out onto the balcony. There were surfers trying to catch a wave on the angry surf, but they were being tossed from their boards. The waves were short and sharp, they were nothing but a nuisance today. Was this telling Lauren that bad weather was about to arrive? She would have to study the weather patterns, as it was always nice to inform the guests what to expect, although all they wanted was sun, surf and more sun. Lauren had two days before she took over her management position, so tomorrow she would spend a couple of hours in reception and familiarise herself with the goings-on. All she had to do now was to wait for her furniture to arrive. She settled in a deckchair and gazed to the horizon, leaving her mind blank, so as not to have any unwanted thoughts popping in. She was oblivious to all around her. She had not bothered to look into any of the apartments, she was used to blanking out what was happening next door. Several of the guests watched with interest at this new person who had suddenly appeared and made herself at home in the deckchair. Was she there for one night, or would she stay for several days? Tomorrow would tell the story.

Lauren was brought out of her daydream by the phone ringing. She jumped up and rushed to answer it; her furniture had arrived, would she make her way down to reception. This she did. The managers agreed to lock off the lift so her belongings could be transported up to level four without any interruptions. The trucking guys carried her gear to the lift and offered to come up and help her lift it into her apartment. This offer she kindly accepted. Once they had gone, all that was left for Lauren to do was to find a place for all her treasures, as these were good memories of her past. The bad ones she had left behind. With each placement she relived the memories; where they were bought, how she had saved to buy them, some with Scott's blessing, others without.

Come darkness, she had everything in its place. How lovely to be able to put things where she liked them, not where he said they had to go. This was the freedom of one's own decision-making, one she had missed. These choices that had been taken from her, now they were available to her again. This brought a sigh of relief; feelings of self-worth were returning. She thought they had completely gone, but they had survived the past traumas, and here they were once again! Her life was only beginning, at age twenty-seven she had to make up for the lost years.

Today, as Lauren had predicted, the weather had changed. It was overcast and dull, even a few spots of rain had appeared, but this didn't dampen her feelings. This was the first day of her new life, so of course she wouldn't let anything petty stand in her way. She looked at her surroundings. It was only then she realised she was on show to the guests in the other apartments on her floor. Because of the shape and positioning of the building so all apartments could have ocean views, there was very little privacy in the living quarters, only when the drapes were drawn. This she would have to remember. The bedrooms were fine, as they faced the back of the building. Not that she was a nosy person, but as manager her eyes were open to anything untoward, as this was expected of her.

After having a bite of lunch, she made her way down to

reception and met with the young lady who was on duty. She was presentable and very obliging with the guests, very much like herself all those years ago. This was how she started in the hospitality industry, first in reception, then she was promoted to the manager's bed … big mistake. This was how she met Scott. He was the resort manager, married and a very handsome, self-confident man. He was a control freak, but this realisation came too late, even after a warning from his wife that she wouldn't be the last, but this she chose to ignore. Lauren was in his clutches for the next ten years, until their receptionist did her a justice and become his lover. She felt sorry for her, so sent out a warning which, like her, she chose to ignore. What was to come next, she had to find out for herself!

Lauren learnt that Anna worked reception at this new resort from Monday to Friday from 7.30am to 5.00pm. Then the managers took over each night to 9.30pm, as well as working the weekends. Lauren knew the more work she did, the more money she made. The hours were going to be a big ask, but she was up for it. She was on a strict savings pattern. At this stage there was no thought of another partner, certainly not! She would carry on the same hours of work the present managers did, until she sorted herself out. She would have the week days off until 5.00pm in which she could relax and forget her worries … but what worries? she asked herself!

She looked through the register to see how many apartments were let permanently and there was six; four were semi-permanent and seven were rentals. This would keep her busy enough. "Can you fill me in on the semi-rentals, Anna?" she asked. "Yes, at this stage they are open, meaning they have not given us a date when they will be vacating. But we have a rule that they must give us a fortnight's notice in advance. There is a couple and their daughter in apartment twelve on your floor, they have been in for a month now. They seem nice people. They come and go a lot, although I very rarely see the daughter." Lauren thanked Anna for that information, as it was useful to know a little of what was going on. She would learn more in due course. She knew as manager, one never became too familiar with the guests, as then favours began to be expected. There always had to be that little aloofness; she had learnt this by past experiences. As they were talking, the couple from apartment twelve appeared at reception, so Anna introduced Lauren as the new manager. "Lauren, this is Mr and Mrs Langlands, they have been with us for a month." "Pleased to meet you, I hope I will see you about often," she replied. They smiled and took their leave. "What age is their daughter?" asked Lauren. "She is a hard one to pick an age for, perhaps eighteen, I don't really know. She is certainly different, doesn't say much, in fact she shies away from any conversation."

Tonight, Lauren had been asked down to have a farewell drink with the managers, as they were leaving tomorrow. They were moving back to their home town of Shepperton. Their management days were over, they just wanted time to themselves. It was all up to Lauren after tomorrow, so last-minute information was being handed over. The groundsman worked six days, but only six hours a day. He would come in on a Sunday if there were any emergencies. "You will find it a bit hectic on your own, as we shared the duties," they told her. "I like being busy, it takes my mind off other things." They thought with this remark, she must have had a broken relationship that she was still getting over. "It's onwards and upwards from here," Lauren told them. Definitely a broken relationship! They said their farewells and Lauren left to go to her apartment.

Today was the first day as manageress of Blue Water Apartments. Lauren was up early as she wanted to say goodbye to the managers as they left. They may have forgotten to tell her something and remembered during the night, so she felt she had to be there to see them off and get any last-minute instructions. Their furniture had left a week earlier when they vacated the manager's apartment so Lauren could move in. Yesterday they packed their wagon with the last of their belongings. There were last-minute goodbyes as they were ready to leave on their road trip. They hugged Lauren and wished her well. There was only one cautionary note on departure. "Watch the young lady in apartment twelve, she is strange," and with this they drove off. Lauren was a little bewildered by this statement. Was this a warning? She would do just that and keep her eye on her.

When Anna arrived to open reception at 7.30am she was surprised to see her boss was already there. "You're up and on the job early," she said to Lauren. "I wanted to be here to say goodbye in case they forgot to tell me something. But they did pass a comment about the young girl in apartment twelve. They said she was strange. Why would they say that?" "Yes, the young lady is different. I don't see her much, she is not a day person, but she is apparently out and about at night." How strange! thought Lauren. She thanked Anna and caught the lift up to her apartment to get herself some breakfast. She opened her drapes, only to reveal another overcast day. Then something caught her eye through one of the glass sliding doors. There was a young person crouched down in a corner, she looked like she was sobbing. Lauren quickly retreated back so she couldn't be seen, then realised this must be the young person from apartment twelve. Why would she be huddled in a corner? she asked herself. She had to have another peep to make sure this was what she had actually witnessed. Yes, there she was, her eyes were not playing tricks on her, but where were her parents? She picked up the phone and rang down to reception. "Anna, the Langlands, have you seen them this morning?" "Yes, they left early but they were on their own, why?" she asked. Lauren decided not to say what she had seen, she would keep it to herself at the moment, so thanked Anna.

Tonight was her first night on reception. Anna had finished at 5.00pm so Lauren was on until 9.30pm. People came and went. Lauren felt a little lost, as she didn't know any of the guests, apart from the Langlands, but of course this would change after she had been here for a couple of months. "Excuse me, could you tell me what apartment the Langlands are in?" With this Lauren looked up to find a middle-aged Asian man enquiring. "Apartment twelve on the fourth floor. Would you like me to ring them and let them know you are here?" "No, thank you, they are expecting me," and he headed to the lift. Lauren didn't know if the parents had come back or if the daughter was on her own. She felt a little concerned, but decided it was none of her business, she could not become involved in other people's lives. Just at that moment, her mind was taken away from apartment twelve as a couple came in off the street wanting an apartment for three nights, as they were going to a wedding. Lauren took them up to have an inspection of the room, with which they were very happy, so they signed the register, paid and received their key. They had come down from Brisbane.

Come 9.30pm Lauren locked up reception and caught

the lift to the fourth floor, where she unlocked her door and went in. Tomorrow was Saturday so she was on reception all day, and hopefully she would meet more of the permanent guests. She went over to the windows to close the drapes and just by chance, no, intentionally glanced into apartment twelve, only to see the Asian man was still there. The lonely figure of the girl was still crouched in the corner, but there didn't seem to be any sign of the parents. Lauren didn't linger, she pulled the drapes for her own privacy, but she did worry for the girl!

She poured herself a glass of red wine, she was still excited about the fact that she had the management rights of this fabulous apartment block. She realised she didn't need Scott to hold her hand, she could make it on her own! Why hadn't she done this years ago instead of suffering? But it took him to do the dirty on her, and this was her only way out. He thought he could keep her and have his bit on the side. But to find out the bit on the side was their receptionist was the means to the end. She hadn't told him where she was going, this was a complete break-away, she never wanted to see him again. She did wonder if he had promoted her to his bed. Was this history repeating itself?

Two months had passed without any problems and she had met most of the other guests as they came and went. Today Mrs Langlands had come to reception to see if a parcel had arrived for her. Lauren noticed she dressed in hippy-type clothes, very modern indeed for a middle-aged lady. She felt she wanted to compliment her on her stylish clothing. "You look lovely today," she told her. "Why, thank you, I do all my shopping at St Vinnies, the Salvation Army thrift shops." This took Lauren by surprise, in fact she was totally shocked. She didn't look like someone who would wear second-hand clothing. "Well, you certainly choose well," was all she could think to say at that moment. She had never met anyone who shopped at St Vinnies, well no one that she knew of. "Could you please ring me when my parcel arrives?" she asked of Lauren. This she promised to do. Just before closing a courier arrived with a package, so she rang the Langlands, who came and collected it straight away.

Each Sunday while on reception, she noticed Mr and Mrs Langlands left the apartment block dressed very stylish, but the daughter was never with them. She did wonder where they went. Then one day during a conversation, Mrs Langlands told Lauren they were Salvation Army members and went to church every Sunday. Now she knew what was happening on Sundays! This was one of her questions answered. But what of the daughter? She was never with them. Lauren had only seen her twice. They were a mystery family; they didn't have a vehicle, several people visited them, but the number of parcels they received was unbelievable. And each time a parcel was delivered, they had to be rung.

One Saturday night after Lauren had closed reception, she waited for the lift to come down to the ground floor. It seemed to be taking its time, then when it did eventually turn up, the door opened and there crouched on the floor was the daughter from apartment twelve. When she saw Lauren she slowly stood up, but was unsteady on her feet. Her eyes were glassy and she seemed dazed. She picked up her backpack and staggered out. "Are you all right?" "Yes" was the only answer she got out of her. Then she opened the door and walked out of the building. Where on earth would she be going at this hour of night, on her own? she wondered. She looked as if she had been drinking. Where were her parents? Before Lauren closed her drapes that night, she looked across at apartment twelve and the Langlands were both there. She was mystified. What a strange set-up, she thought, should she be concerned? No, it was none of her business, she told herself. They were not causing a disturbance to anyone, but she would keep her eye on them!

Several months had passed without any incidents and Lauren was run off her feet. She had only managed to take a couple of mornings away from the place in six months, but this she didn't mind, as she was still finding her way. Once she was more organised, she would take more time off! Her guests in apartment twelve were still with her, but she did wonder how they could afford to pay the rent, as neither seemed to work, although they were out and about a lot. The Asian guy was still turning up regularly, and this was a worry, as sometimes the daughter was there on her own. Then one Friday night, just as Lauren was closing reception, she looked up to see the daughter hurrying out the front entrance door, with her backpack on. She wasn't sure if she had been spotted, so she waited a bit then she decided to see in what direction she went, just out of curiosity. Lauren walked down the pathway to the front street, but she was nowhere to be seen. That is strange, she thought. She could see for miles as the lights lit the street from both ways, but it was empty. Where had she gone? Obviously not out onto the street. By now it was too late, so she would have to wait until next time. And why was she always carrying a backpack?

Tonight, as she was lying in bed, her imagination was running wild. So many bizarre thoughts were flooding her brain. Was she a lady of the night? Surely not, as she never looked appealing, but was her façade hidden in her backpack? Did she have a night job? But she wouldn't go to work if she had been drinking. With all these thoughts in her mind she dropped off to sleep, her brain had shut down. When she woke the next morning, her mind was still focused on the daughter. A mystery, indeed it was.

It was Sunday again, the Langlands were off to church, nothing had changed with their routine. The daughter, as usual, was not with them. People came and went and the day seemed to pass quickly. Later in the afternoon two parcels were brought in by a courier to be delivered to apartment twelve. Lauren did the usual and rang as soon as they were delivered, and they were collected straight away. Thank goodness it was closing time, so she locked up reception and went to the lift. The light was on showing that it was at the fourth floor. Now was her chance — Lauren hurried to the entrance, walked outside and stood behind a bush, in wait. True to her expectations out came the daughter with her backpack, but she didn't walk down the path to the street, instead she took the path that led to the beach. Oh, that is why I lost her the other night, but why would she be going onto the beach in the dark? That would be dangerous on her own, she thought. This was enough for tonight, as she didn't have a torch, so back inside she went. The mystery was deepening and the plot thickening. Then it came to her attention that several parcels had been delivered today. Was there a connection? As she closed her drapes, she had a peep to see if the parents were home, and indeed they were. Suddenly it came to her attention that the apartment always had someone in it, it was never vacated by everyone at the same time. This was why the daughter never went anywhere with her parents. When they were out, she was at home, and vice versa ... but why?

While in reception tonight, Lauren noticed the Asian

guy walk straight to the lift, so she had a look to see what floor it stopped at and true to form, the fourth floor. She had never thought to ask Anna if she had seen him visiting the Langlands during the day, but she would ask her tomorrow. Another day had come to a close and Lauren was waiting for the lift to go to her apartment. When it stopped, out walked the daughter with her backpack, and she was none too steady on her feet. Her hair looked matted, she was certainly no lady of the night, nor would she be going to work in that condition. But where was she going? Lauren caught the lift going back up. She unlocked her apartment door and walked straight to the window. The drapes in apartment twelve were partially drawn, but she could see the Asian visitor was still there. As she reached to draw her drapes, she got the shock of her life: the bench-top of the island bar was covered in wads of notes, all in neat piles. So much money. Where did it come from? The Asian man was counting the money. 'What the hell?' were the first words that came to Lauren's mind. Where did all that money come from? Why was Mrs Langlands buying second-hand clothes at St Vinnies when she could afford to buy new ones? So many scenarios were running through her mind. How? Why? But nothing made sense any more. What was going on in that apartment? It was almost sinister, all that money! She quickly closed the drapes for fear she might be seen to be spying on them, which of course she was!

The next shift that Anna was on, Lauren asked her if she had seen an Asian guy coming and going. She assured her that he was a regular, but she didn't know who he was visiting as he went straight to the lift, he never came to reception. She asked Anna to watch when he next came to see what floor he got off on, as she had to be sure that was the only floor he was visiting. Would she tell Anna what she had seen? No, it was better kept under wraps until she figured what was going on. She did ask her to ring her when parcels were delivered to the Langlands.

It was time to hatch a plan. She had to know where the daughter was going at night, so the next delivery to the Langlands was her clue as to when the daughter would next leave the building. This, of course, would be at night. She would ask Anna to stay on and work her shift and she would wait in the sand dunes to see where she went. It wasn't long before a call came from Anna to say there had been a delivery, she had rung the Langlands and they were on their way down to collect it. With this, Lauren arranged for Anna to do a double shift tonight, then she could have the whole day off tomorrow.

Just on dark, Lauren left the building with a torch and picked a vantage point in the sand dunes where she could see the daughter as she came down the steps onto the beach. She didn't know which direction she would be heading, so she stayed close enough that she could follow her either way. Then it all happened. Down the steps she came with her backpack, walking in the direction Lauren was hiding, but she kept to the water's edge for a few hundred yards then she veered up towards the sand dunes. Then she hesitated and looked around before approaching two sticks that were crisscrossed and sticking out of the sand. Lauren saw her stop by the sticks, which looked like they were there for a specific reason. She knelt down and started digging with her hands, all the time keeping watch. She took off her backpack and lifted something out, then hurriedly buried it. She stood up and retreated back the way she had come. Suddenly a dreadful thought flooded Lauren's brain. No, it couldn't be, no way, but reality took

over. Was she witnessing a drug drop-off? Was she plant-
ing drugs for someone to pick up? Was that drug money
she had seen in the Langlands' apartment? Who was the
Asian guy? Was he a money launderer and all those parcels
that were delivered was that how they got the drugs? Lauren sat frozen to the spot when she realised one of her
apartments was perhaps being used as a drug distribution
centre.

As she was about to leave, a man came down from the
dunes and went to where the sticks were. He knelt down
and started digging, then he lifted a parcel from the sand
and reached in his pocket and took something out and put
it in the hole he had dug. He covered it, then stood up and
went on his way. Now she had witnessed a drop-off and a
pick-up. She waited for a few minutes then shakily snuck
along the sand dunes. She was petrified, as she had read
what happened to those who interfered in the drug scene.
Now she felt she was part of it. What would she do? No
way could she tell Anna, that would bring her into it. She
didn't want her to be involved, in case of retribution. No,
Anna must not know what was happening.

When she arrived back, Anna had locked up and gone
home. She was pleased that she had given her the day
off tomorrow, as she would not have to face her. Lauren
needed time to think things over in the protection of her
own environment. At least when she was in reception, she
could see who came and went, but this was of little com-
fort to her now. How would she feel when she next had
to face the Langlands? As she made her way to the lift,
she could see it had just left the fourth floor. Who was
she going to meet? As the door opened, out stepped the
daughter with her backpack. Lauren was in shock. Where
would she be going this time? Then she remembered the

pick-up guy had buried something. Was she going to retrieve what he had left? Was it money, perhaps payment for the drugs? She felt sick, this poor girl was the drug courier. Now Lauren knew why she was shaky and had glassy eyes — it wasn't alcohol, she was an addict! But her parents, why would they feed their daughter drugs? Then a terrible thought came to her. Perhaps she wasn't their daughter, perhaps she was someone else's daughter who had been lured into the seedy underworld.

She let herself into her apartment and walked over to the windows and pulled close her drapes. She had seen enough, she didn't want to see anything else tonight, as she could hardly cope with what she had discovered. Time for a wine, she convinced herself. She needed something to relax, as now she carried another unwanted burden, one with so many disastrous consequences! What if someone had seen her, what could she expect to happen to her? In all her ten years in the hospitality industry, never had she encountered anything as dangerous as drugs, so she was out of her depth. Should she tell the police? Would the Langlands know it was her that had reported them? If so, what would they do to her? It was all too much — she burst into tears. Where to from here?

This morning Lauren was in reception at 7.30am. She was still reeling from last night and prayed that the Langlands didn't come near her today. She didn't know how she would react towards them. But it didn't take long for her worst fear to be realised. Mrs Langlands made her way to reception and was on for a chat. This is unusual, thought Lauren. "Today I'm on my way to St Vinnies to do some shopping, as they have a sale and all the clothes are heavily reduced, so I'm hoping to pick up some bargains." Before Lauren realised, she had opened her mouth and out flowed her thoughts. "But why do you shop there? Other shops have bargains and their clothes are new." "We are great supporters of the Salvation Army so we like to buy from them. They do so much good for all communities here in Australia and overseas. You must come along one day," she suggested. Never before had she been so friendly. Did she know something? Fear crept in. Was she trying to lure her away so she could get some sort of revenge? "Perhaps, one day," Lauren answered in a quivering voice. "Are you all right?" she asked. What could Lauren say? She was petrified and it was showing. She had to pull herself together and act normal but that was easier said than done! "I just overindulged a little last night, but I'll come right." "Were you celebrating something special?" she asked. This was becoming a nightmare. When was she going to let up and stop asking questions? What was this leading up to, did she know something? The only reply she could think of and blurted out was "It was my birthday," which of course wasn't true. "Happy birthday, Lauren, of course you should celebrate," she replied, then she took her leave. Never had she wanted to get rid of someone so quickly as Mrs Langlands. She tugged at her hair, nearly pulling it out at the roots in frustration. She was frightened and it was showing! Here she was in her own apartment block and she felt unsafe, all because of the drug situation.

Suddenly she was disturbed by a cough and she looked up to see a courier guy standing at reception with a parcel, no guessing who that was for! "Please see that this is delivered to apartment twelve straight away," he asked. "Yes, I will ring this very minute," and with this she picked up the phone. "Mr Langlands, a parcel has arrived addressed to you." With this the courier man left satisfied. It was only a matter of minutes before Mr Langlands came down and picked it up. It was only then that Lauren realised that he was quite a pleasant-looking man. He thanked her and re-entered the lift. Tonight, there would probably be another drop-off by the daughter, Lauren presumed. She would stay in reception until she came down with her backpack, and if so, what she had presumed would be verified. The day the drugs were delivered, they were disposed of just as quickly, in case of a police raid. Just before 5.00pm she saw Mrs Langlands arriving with a lot of parcels, so she lifted the receiver off the telephone and talked into thin air, and gave her a wave hoping she would go straight to the lift, which indeed she did.

After Lauren closed reception at 9.30, she could see that the lift was stopped at the fourth floor. She waited until it came down to the foyer and when it opened, standing there in a daze was the daughter decked out with her back-pack. Lauren smiled at her, she didn't want her to feel she had noticed anything unusual. The daughter dropped her head down and hurried out the entrance door. So yes, this confirmed the day the parcels arrived, there was a delivery. She had to talk to someone, but who? She let herself into her apartment, pulled the drapes and fell into her favourite chair. Who could she talk to? She was frightened, and this showed up today in front of Mrs Langlands. It was almost a display of stupidity and she had told lies, this was not like her, this was another person! She was not in control! If she didn't go to the police and the apartments were raided, would she be charged as an accessory to a crime? This was a serious situation, yes, she had no option but to go to the police. She had a duty to protect her guests and, of course, herself. Now that she had made a positive decision, tomor-row morning she would be off to the police station.

Lauren stopped off at reception to let Anna know she would be away for most of the day, but would be back for her shift. She caught the lift to the basement carpark and got into her car. She was nervous, as she had never had anything to do with the police in the past. What was she going to say, how was she going to approach the subject? But at least she had actual evidence, well, in her head, that something untoward was going on. After parking her car several blocks away from the police station, she decided to walk just in case someone was watching her, or she was being followed. This was the effect all this was having on her — she was becoming paranoid.

At the desk stood a stern-looking policewoman. "How can I help you?" she asked. Lauren was silent for a moment, then she spoke. "I wish to speak with someone in the drug squad." She looked at Lauren. "I will get one of our officers to speak with you, just take a seat." She could see this young lady was nervous. After five minutes she was asked to come through to a private office where a man was seated. "This is Detective Flynn, he will speak with you," then she closed the door and left. "How can I help you?" he asked. Lauren didn't know where to start. The tears started — was this because some of the pressure was going to be released? She tried to pull herself together. Once she settled, she told him all she knew. "So, you have seen all this yourself? How much money do you think was on the bench?" he asked. Lauren told him she didn't know, but there were many bundles, she felt frightened so she pulled the drapes. "And you followed the daughter and watched her burying something in the sand, then saw the pick-up. Would you be able to explain where this happened?" Lauren told him she would only be too pleased to co-operate. "But I don't want the police to come to the apartment block for fear of retaliation," she told him. "What we will do is send a plain-clothed detective to your apartment as a cover-up. No one will know what is happening, he could just be a man friend. You obviously live on your own?" Lauren verified this. "I'm sorry, I don't even know your name?" he asked. "I'm Lauren, I am the manageress of the Blue Water Apartments." "Tomorrow I will send a detective to your building to meet with you, Lauren, his name will be Mike. You can discuss this with him and he can get a feel for the situation. Do you mind if he spends time in your apartment, then he can keep his eye on what is happening next door? Is this okay with you?" Lauren assured Detective Flynn that she would be happy to have some protection, as she was fearful of what might happen next. They both stood up and shook hands. "Thank you, Lauren, you have done the right thing by coming to us." With this she left the station feeling a little more relieved.

She walked to a nearby café to have some lunch and a cup of strong coffee. While she was sitting there, she was sure she saw Scott walk by. Surely not, he didn't know where she was. What would he be doing here? She hadn't told him anything, so he wouldn't know of her whereabouts. Who would have told him? Was it coincidence, or had he tracked her down? She didn't need any more distractions; her life was in enough turmoil. A tear slipped down her cheek so she quickly wiped it away. Was it a tear of despair or one of relief? ... She didn't know any more!

Lauren couldn't really settle into shopping, too much was going on in her mind. She decided enough was enough, she would head home for a rest before she took over reception at 5.oopm. After parking her car, she caught the lift straight up to the fourth floor; she didn't want to stop at reception, she needed time out. Just as she stepped out of the lift, she noticed the daughter from apartment twelve crouched on the floor. Before she could stop herself, she asked, "Are you okay?" Tears were streaming down her face. "Can I help you?" Lauren asked again. At that very moment the door opened, and Mr Langlands pulled her inside. Lauren hurried to her apartment and let herself in. Oh my God, did he hear me questioning his daughter? she wondered. Now what was going to happen? She collapsed into her chair. Tomorrow couldn't come quickly enough, that was when the detective called Mike was going to arrive. She couldn't have a drink to steady her nerves, as she was due in reception in a short while. Lauren closed her eyes and wished for everything to disappear. Then she remembered she thought she had seen her ex Scott. Perhaps she had just imagined it, among all her fears. She closed her eyes and dozed off, until she was brought back to life by the phone ringing.

It was Anna checking to see if she was home. There was someone in reception asking for her. She looked at the time, it was four o'clock, she only had an hour. "I'll be down in a minute," she said, then hung up. Had the detective arrived early? This was a happy thought. When she arrived at reception she was surprised, but not happy, to see her ex Scott. It must have been him she saw earlier! "Hello, Lauren, you have a nice place here, I've missed you." "What happened to Lucy?" she asked, she couldn't help herself. "She has gone, she found someone else. It wasn't until you left that I realised how much you meant to me," he told her, trying to win her over. "Well, I'm sorry, Scott, I have moved on. I have a life of my own and I'm happy. I bought the management rights to this property, this is my new life." Scott looked disappointed, he thought

Lauren would fall straight back into his arms. "I have to take over reception now, so you will have to go," she told him. "I'll come back tomorrow and we can have a talk then." She didn't know how to answer this, as there was so much still going on in her mind. On that note he left. Anna had been privy to this conversation, so she didn't mention it to her boss, as she could see she was upset.

She passed on to Lauren what had happened on her shift, now it was time for her to finish for the day. "See you in the morning, Lauren," she called as she left the building. Poor Lauren now had another problem, one she wished she didn't have and that was her ex Scott. Strangely she felt no emotions towards him, she had left them behind when she walked out. What had happened to Lucy? Lauren had a quiet smile to herself. Had she discovered his controlling ways? She didn't last long, she was sensible, she had escaped before it was too late. Now he wanted her back! Not a chance, he had blown their friendship by bedding her!

Reception was quiet tonight. She looked to see if any parcels had been delivered for apartment twelve, as all inward mail or deliveries were recorded, but no, there was nothing. This meant there would be no drop-offs tonight. It would give her a chance to relax before her ordeal with the detective tomorrow and, of course, her meeting with Scott. She wondered how Scott had found her. Hopefully tonight she would have a good sleep, as she felt she had lightened her burden a little by going to the police. It now meant she would not be implicated in any drug raids on the apartments. She was glad that was all sorted.

# 2

# Detective Mike

This morning Lauren was up early in preparation for a busy day. She rang down to Anna and asked her to send Scott up when he arrived. She presumed he would arrive earlyish, as he would be anxious to know how she was coping. Well, he would soon learn that she no longer needed him, she could make it on her own, this she had proven. As she was having breakfast there was a knock on her door. She got up and unlocked it and there stood Scott. Lauren invited him in and as he passed her, he stole a kiss. This all happened before she realised. "You look well, Lauren; this position must suit you." "What are you up to now?" she asked. "I have finished my position at the Coral Reef Resort. I thought a change was in order. I was actually hoping we could team up again and manage something together, we were a good team." "Yes, Scott, we were a good team, but you couldn't control your wondering eye with younger receptionists. It happened to me, then Lucy. Who will be next? But not any more, we are finished, I'm happy with my life, our time together ended when you bedded Lucy. I have no feelings left for you," she told him. Scott was not prepared for this, he didn't think she had it in her to go it alone, he thought she needed him. "But I still have feelings for you, Lauren, we had ten good years together. I made a mistake, Lucy was just a fleeting attraction". "Scott, that is how we started, I was just like Lucy, a young receptionist who foolishly fell for the manager, only I stuck with you, but Lucy obviously learnt early in the piece and got out before she felt trapped. She was the sensible one." "What do you mean by that?" he asked. "You are a control freak, Scott, I should have left years ago, but Lucy did me a favour. I am now free and it feels good. I want you to forget me and move on like I have done." Lauren felt good saying this. Scott was shocked by this revelation, he didn't see himself as a controlling person, but then he wouldn't, he was the manager, she was just the receptionist. "Do you have a new partner?" he wanted to know. "No, I'm not interested at the moment, perhaps one day, who knows?" "Would you like a coffee?" she offered. "Yes, please, Lauren, that would be nice." He thought if he stayed a little longer, she might look at him in a different light. She was hurting, he could see this, but only in his own mind. They chattered about their life — there had been good times and it took her mind off other things.

They were disturbed by the phone, it was Anna. "There is a gentleman here by the name of Mike, he said you were expecting him. Shall I send him up?" "Yes, please, Anna." "I'm sorry, Scott, you will have to leave. I have a visitor coming to see me, we have important business to discuss." With this he stood up and took Lauren in his arms. "Please let me into your life again," he pleaded. "Let me go, we can be no more than just friends," Lauren let him know. There was a knock on the door, she broke free from his arms and went to answer it. "Hi, Lauren, I'm Mike," and he put out his hand to shake hers. She was shocked, there before her stood a hunk of a man. She invited him in. 'This is my ex Scott, he was just leaving," and with that she showed him to the door. He told her he would like to see her again. He was upset, who was this guy, what business did they have to discuss, why did they want to get rid of him? He reluctantly left, but vowed he would be back. "Sorry, that was my ex-partner," explained Lauren.

Mike introduced himself as an undercover detective who worked with the drug squad. He had been briefed at the station about what was going on, but he really needed to hear the full story from her. Lauren explained what was happening, but she couldn't get it in her head what the Langlands' association with the Salvation Army was. "They are cunning operators, they are using this charity as a cover-up. Who would expect members of the Salvation Army to be dealing in drugs? This is the perfect alibi for them." "But I am worried about the daughter, I have found her in vulnerable situations at times, I think she is a user?" stated Lauren. "I would be surprised if she is their daughter, she will be their drug mule. They will have set up this nice little family situation to throw people off their scent. They know all the tricks of the trade, they are not silly people, by any means. Can we see their apartment from here?" he asked. "Yes, if you walk over to the glass sliding doors, you can see into their apartment. I can't understand why they don't fully pull their drapes." "Sometimes these are the little mistakes they make, thank goodness you are observant as to what is happening around you. Come out onto the balcony with me so I can get a feel for the situation." They walked out through the doors and looked at the view. Mike had to appear as a friend of Lauren's so as not to cause any suspicion as to why he was there. He knew how to handle these situations. His eyes diverted to the suspects' windows, yes, he could see in, there was a lady and a man standing talking. Mike sensed they had seen him, so he quickly took Lauren in his arms and cuddled her to give them the impression they were lovers. Two could play at the cover-up game! Lauren was startled but did not protest, it felt good to be in someone's arms again, even if it was a good-looking stranger. He walked her inside, then apologised for his behaviour, but he had to squash any doubts that the neighbours might have had.

Lauren had asked Anna to call her first if any parcels were for apartment twelve before she rang the Langlands to come and collect them. It didn't take long before the call came through. "Hi, Lauren, the couriers have delivered two parcels." She thanked Anna. "Mike, a delivery has just been made so tonight there will be a drop-off. The daughter usually comes down around the time I close reception, about 9.30pm. What do you think you might do?" she asked. "I will have to be discreet, I can't risk my cover to be blown now that we are on to them. I will come down to you when you lock up. This is the first part of my first mission, as I would like to see this young lady, then I know who I'm dealing with. If you give me a key to your apartment, I'll come back about 9.15."

At five o'clock Lauren came down to take over at reception. "Wow, what a catch, where did you meet him?" quizzed Anna. This took Lauren by surprise, she had to think quickly. "I've known him from way back, we have just met up again." Anna voiced her approval! She knew not to mention her ex, as there seemed to be an air of coolness between them. "See you tomorrow," she called as she left. Just the thought of Mike made Lauren's heart race, but why? she asked herself. She had only just met him today, she knew nothing about him, perhaps he was married? She had a bit of bookwork to finish before she closed up. Mike had arrived and gone up to her apartment. Just before 9.30pm she saw the lift leaving floor four, who would be in it this time? When it arrived at the foyer and the door opened there was Mike and the glazed-eyed daughter with her backpack.

Mike got out and came over and took Lauren in his arms, as if to embrace her. He had to look convincing so no suspicions were aroused. But really, the state the daughter was in, she would not have noticed what was going on around her. "Hi, love, I have been waiting for you," he whispered to Lauren. With this the daughter passed them by and left the building. "You are right, Lauren, that girl is an addict. That will be why they recruited her, they will keep up the drugs for her and by doing this they are in control. She will do anything for her next fix. No way will she be their daughter, she is a drug mule." "What is a drug mule?" asked Lauren. "That is another name used in the underworld for a drug courier. It is so sad for the young kids that get caught up in that scene. That is why we have to get the dealers and put them away," he told her. "Are you going to follow her?" Mike assured her he would take on one thing at a time, this was a delicate situation. If they got a whiff of what was going on, then they would move their operation elsewhere. "I just had to get a bearing on the girl and see where she fitted in the chain, now I'm happy," he said. He told Lauren it was going to be a drawn-out process, but they needed all the available evidence if they wanted to put them away. Dealing with drug dealers and their sidekicks was a complicated job, as they were usually one step ahead of the police, but hopefully not this time! Lauren invited Mike up for a cup of coffee, which he gratefully accepted.

Over the next couple of weeks Mike popped in and out of her apartment. He now had a clear picture of the Langlands and their so-called daughter. The next person he was keen to see was the Asian guy, but this would have to be in the secrecy of Lauren's apartment. Mike couldn't afford to be recognised, as he was afraid he might have encountered him on a previous drug raid. Lauren was to ring him when he next appeared. Today was that day. Anna rang to say the Asian guy was on his way up to the fourth floor. Straight away Lauren phoned Mike, he would be there in a flash. She peeped into their apartment and she could see them all sitting on stools around the island bench. Was the money going to come out? she wondered. She moved away and prayed that Mike would get here quickly! True to his word, he arrived in extra fast time. He walked over to the window and peeped next door. He never expected to see what was before his eyes. He was shocked— there laid out on the bench were bundles of notes. He had come to identify the Asian guy but he got more than he bargained for! He studied the visitor, but he was not known to him. This was a new player to the game, but they were popping up everywhere, it was such a lucrative business. This was definitely a drug payment, so now he knew they were dealing with a sizable drug syndicate. He would hunt them down and put them away!

Lauren was enjoying Mike being there, it was only now she was realising she had missed male company. There had been several more incidents when they were forced into each other's arms, but it always ended in an apology from Mike. One day, she secretly hoped it would be for real. Feelings were being stirred in her body; they had lay dormant for a long time, but now they were coming back with a vengeance. She started taking more notice of herself, her cheeks had a healthy glow and tingling sensations were forever reminding her she was in need of love. They had had a lot of conversations, and he had let slip that he was still single. This did not escape her attention!

The next morning Lauren received a phone call from Mike asking her to come to the police station, as they had put a strategy in place and wanted to see if she could arrange for it to proceed. He wouldn't mention anything over the phone, but if she could come down, then they would hold a meeting. Upon her arrival she was shown into a special room where there were five men seated around a boardroom table. "Guys, this is Lauren, she is the manager of the apartment block where our targets are operating from. We have come up with a plan to bug their apartment, Lauren, and we would need an apartment below the targets for a couple of weeks so we can monitor their movements. The force is prepared to pay rent, can you arrange this for us? Do your girls service their apartment?" asked Mike. "No, the Langlands pick up clean linen every Saturday and leave their used linen outside their door and the girls pick it up. The apartment has never been left unattended, there is always someone there." "We want our guys to bug the apartment, so we can have actual physical evidence they are drug dealers. What we propose to do is to have undercover police disguised as bug exterminators. This way all the apartments will have to be evacuated with a four-hour stand-down period, which will give us time to set up the listening device. We have done this before and it has been successful. All we require from you is to let each apartment guest know a date and time this will be happening. Is this possible?" asked Mike. Lauren agreed to this, but one thing was worrying her. "Why haven't you followed the daughter and seen where they bury the drugs?" "We are not worried about the mules or the pick-ups, we want the kingpins, the dealers. Once we get them then the chain falls apart. They are the ones becoming wealthy at the demise of innocent lives. We have to destroy them, lock them up, take them out of society." Now Lauren understood.

Notice had gone out to all the apartments asking them to vacate for four hours to allow the bug exterminators to come in and fumigate. This would be happening next Monday at ten o'clock. Lauren received a call from the Langlands asking if they could be exempt. Lauren had to explain it was Health and Safety regulations and the whole building had to be fumigated at the same time. Once told how it worked, they seem to understand and they dropped their protest. Surely, she had given them plenty of time to hide whatever they didn't want to be found. It was imperative the bug be planted. They had to be stopped!

# 3

# Police surveillance begins

This morning when Anna came to work there was a guest waiting at reception. She had been for an early morning walk along the beach, and just down from the apartment block, she had found a backpack lying on the sand. It was wet. She wondered if it belonged to someone staying in the apartments. She would leave it with Anna in case anyone enquired about it. Anna thanked her and put it in the office at the back of reception, as she was busy with checkouts. The bug exterminators were moving into their apartment at nine o'clock. In all, it was going to be a busy morning. Anna hadn't been told who the bug guys were, and this Lauren felt terrible about, but no one was to know. This was a police matter, and had to stay just that. She still knew nothing about the drugs, as Lauren didn't want her to be burdened with any of this. Right to plan the bug guys arrived with their equipment and were given the key to apartment nine on the third floor. They set up their listening device, now all they had to do was plant the bug in the above apartment. Lauren had requested that Anna ring her when she saw the Langlands leaving, which was scheduled for ten o'clock.

Lauren waited for the call. True to form it came through at 9.45am but only Mr and Mrs Langlands were seen leaving, their daughter was not with them. Lauren thought this was strange. Where would she be? Surely she wasn't still in the apartment? She went to the apartment the drug squad were occupying and told them that the daughter had not been seen leaving. They were eager to get on with the task at hand, so made their way to the above floor, to apartment twelve. They knocked several times but there was no answer, so they let themselves in. They searched each room, but no daughter! Now it was all clear for them to set up their device.

Meanwhile Lauren went to reception to speak with Anna. "Did the Langlands' daughter leave the building earlier this morning?" "No, she hasn't left since I came on duty, perhaps she left before I came?" With this Lauren went into her office, it was only then that Anna remembered the backpack. "Lauren, a guest found a backpack on the beach this morning while out walking. She saw it lying on the sand, then a gust of wind came and blew it along, so she anchored it with a stick, thinking someone had forgotten it and would come back to collect it. But when she came back an hour later it was still there, so she brought it in here, thinking it might belong to a guest, so I put it in your office." As soon as Lauren saw the backpack, she knew who it belonged to. As she picked it up water trickled from it all over the carpet. "Anna, was it wet when it was handed in?" she asked. "Yes, the lady said it must have got wet when the waves came in." With this Lauren left with the backpack and caught the lift to her apartment. She rang Mike to come straight away.

When he arrived, she showed him the backpack and explained how it came to be in her care. "Mike, I am worried about the daughter, where she is; this belonged to her. She has not been seen today. Her parents left the building, but she was not with them." Mike unzipped it and inside were individual packets, all wrapped in foil. He took out his knife and cut the corner off one of the packets and inside was a white crystallised substance. He knew exactly what it was. Now they had proof that they were dealing in drugs. But what of the girl? She hadn't obviously done her drop-off, something must have happened to her while she was on her way there. But why were the drugs still in the backpack? If someone was following, surely they would have searched her backpack? Mike could not offer any exclamation as to what might have happened, and this left him worried. It looked like foul play, but why hadn't the pack been taken, or the contents removed? He suggested perhaps an aerial search would be the first place to start. Lauren felt sick; this more or less pointed to the fact that something bad had happened. Mike put a call through to headquarters and expressed his concern as to what might have happened to the missing girl. Everything was escalating! The drug squad were bugging the Langlands' apartment, now the daughter was missing. What else could go wrong? A search would have to be conducted under secret surveillance, so as not to jeopardise the pending drug bust. But why hadn't the daughter been reported as missing?

Once the apartment was bugged the drug squad left, as all they had to do now was wait and see what eventuated! Meanwhile, the rest of the men carried out the bug extermination. They had done this many times before to catch criminals, so it had to be done in a professional way. No suspicious behaviour was to be displayed, as this was a delicate situation, one that had to yield results. These drug dealers had to be gotten rid of, taken off the streets and put in cells, even that was too good for them! Mike told Lauren he would head back to the station and arrange an air search of the sea, just in case she had drowned. "But why would that happen?" she asked. "If she was full of drugs she could have been disorientated and walked into the water. It just seems strange that nothing was taken from her pack, this practically rules out foul play. I'll call you later and let you know what is happening." Lauren went down in the lift with him to talk to Anna. "If the lady who found the backpack asks about it, please tell her it was picked up by its owner." Anna looked at her and wondered why, but just let it pass. She hadn't put two and two together, but then, she hadn't seen the daughter much as she was a night person, so the backpack didn't mean anything to her.

It was that time for Lauren to take over reception. The Langlands hadn't come back yet, which surprised her, as she thought with their daughter missing, they would be back as soon as time allowed. But this did not happen. She busied herself with her bookwork, but her thoughts drifted to Mike. She knew she had feelings for him and with each day they steadily grew. She longed for him to take her in his arms, without being followed by an apology. Suddenly she was woken from her daydream by a voice that was familiar to her. She looked up and there stood Scott. "Hi, Lauren, I had to go back to finalise my management changeover, but now I'm back. I've missed you." "I'm sorry, Scott, I'm working, will you please go." "I want to rent an apartment for a couple of days?" he asked. Lauren had to tell him they had no vacancies, which was the truth. "Okay, I'll find somewhere nearby. Catch you later," then he left. She had hoped she had seen the last of him, but this was not so, he still hadn't let go. He was the last person she would be interested in. It took her ten years to break free, she would never go back there ever again. "Hi, Lauren, is our apartment ready?" and there at the desk stood the Langlands. "Yes, the bug men have finished all the apartments, so it is all go." They thanked her and caught the lift. Not a word was said about their daughter. How strange, thought Lauren.

Just as she was locking up, she saw Mike arriving, so she waited and they went up in the lift together. He was getting off on the third floor, so told her he would be along shortly. Lauren's heart started beating faster, she was excited. She showered and changed into a low-cut dress that showed off her breasts, not to bold, but bold enough, she thought. She looked flushed and her cheeks were scarlet instead of pink. She hoped this wasn't a giveaway. Perhaps they would settle back to pink before he arrived? She poured herself a wine to help relax, then nestled into her favourite chair. This was the happiest she had felt in a long while. Was it the thought of Mike that stirred up these feelings within her?

It wasn't long before there was a knock at the door, so she called for him to come in. He walked over to where she was sitting, and asked her if he could join her in a wine, so walked over to the bench and brought the bottle and a glass over. "I'm off duty tonight, so a wine is in order," he said. They toasted each other, then he told Lauren she looked lovely tonight. "The boys have settled in and are waiting for things to happen. Tomorrow morning there will be a helicopter search of the beach and sand dunes. We held off today for fear of upsetting our plans here. It will just appear as a routine shark-spotting exercise, but on board will be a team of police with special search equipment. I am really worried for the girl," he said, as he expressed his concern. "Do you think she has walked into the water and drowned?" asked Lauren. "It points to that, as nothing was taken from her backpack. I think the Langlands will write her off, by thinking she has absconded with the drugs. They can't report her missing for fear of their own operation being uncovered. They have no idea that we have the backpack, so we are one up on them. We will have to wait and see what is uncovered tomorrow with the search. Let us forget about this for a moment and you tell me about yourself."

Lauren didn't know where to start. She looked at Mike. What would she tell him? But before she could work out where to start, Mike asked, "What about your ex, are you still friends?" Lauren explained about her life with him and his controlling ways, and now that she was free, she had found happiness again. "He wants me back in his life, but I will never go there. Once I left, that was the end," she said as tears ran down her face. Mike came over and lifted her from her chair and held her in his arms. "I'm sorry, Mike," she sobbed. "It's okay to cry, Lauren, you have been through a lot lately." He held on to her; he had wanted to do this after their first meeting, but he knew she was just getting over a broken relationship. She needed time to heal. She cuddled into him and felt safe in his arms. Then her body started to tingle, she wanted him to make love to her. Would it be wrong for her to ask? Suddenly courage prevailed! "Mike, please make love to me. I am ready, my feelings have laid dormant for a long time, but since meeting you they have come alive. Let me share them with you, please take me?" she pleaded. "Are you sure, Lauren, that you are ready for this? I have feelings for you, but thought you were still getting over your ex. That is why I have been holding back," he whispered. "Then what are we waiting for?" she asked, and with this, she unzipped her dress and let it drop on the carpet. There she stood in her bra and undies. This was enough encouragement to bring Mike on, so he picked her up and carried her through to her bedroom, where he lay her on the bed and undid her bra. He caressed her firm breasts and her belly letting his hands slide down to her buttocks, which he massaged as he kissed her body. He skilfully slid down her knickers, then excitement took over, but he was still fully clothed. He fumbled with his zipper, his jeans didn't want to part from his body, so he jumped up and down trying to dislodge them. Lauren was watching and burst into laughter. "Fancy keeping a lover waiting," she teased him. She didn't have to wait a minute longer, he was ready for all she had to offer. Excitement took over their bodies, they both wanted the same thing, to love and be loved and now it was happening. It was impromptu and unplanned, but who cared, the feelings were there and they spoke volumes. Lauren felt complete, never had she felt this before with her ex. She had let her feelings take over. To think she had asked Mike to take her, how presumptuous was that of her? But it added to the excitement. Thank God he wanted her, otherwise she would have felt terribly embarrassed.

They both dropped off to sleep and neither woke until 8.30am. It was Lauren who woke first and when she saw Mike was still in her bed, she cuddled into him. What a fun night they had! She felt fulfilled and happy. She leaned over and kissed him, telling him it was time to wake up. When he realised what had happened last night, he wanted to stay tucked up in bed with her, that was until he looked at his watch and saw what time it was. He was meant to be at work, as he had a search to arrange. "You little minx, you will get me sacked for being late," he said, as he hurriedly dressed. "But I have to admit it was worth it, thank you, Lauren, I'll be back for more," and with these words he let himself out.

As Lauren was getting out of the shower, the phone rang so she hurried to answer it. It was Anna. "A courier has dropped off two parcels for the Langlands. Lauren thanked her and finished dressing. Now what was going to happen? Who would do the drug drop-offs? Tonight was going to be very interesting, that was until Lauren's mind went back to the supposed daughter. Where was she, was she floating somewhere out to sea? How sad to have no one and not be missed by anyone, but she was someone's daughter. Someone must care somewhere. She had been used as a drug mule and now that she was missing, no one cared — how very sad! Deep down, Lauren hoped she had been spared, but only time would tell! To think this was happening here, in her apartment block, what a shock. But one had to remember, this was, after all, Surfers Paradise, the place that everyone wanted to be part of. This included people from all walks of life: the high society snobs and the out-of-sorts down-and-outers, all trying to live off one another. There was something here for everyone. Yes, how true, she had found Mike.

As she was deep in thought the phone rang again. "Hi, Lauren, Scott is here to see you, will I send him up?" She was not expecting this, but she would see him and put a stop to it. "Yes, okay, Anna." Today would be the end of Scott and her forever. When she heard the knock at the door she went and opened it. Suddenly she was in his arms being controlled once again. Lauren struggled free, she was angry. "Stop this, Scott, we are finished, get this into your thick skull, I have no feelings for you." "But we were lovers, Lauren, how can you forget the times we had together?" he pleaded. "I have forgotten, it has all been erased, in fact I now have a new lover and am very happy." Then he spotted the two half-empty glasses of wine on the coffee table. "Why are they not finished?" he wanted to know. Right, she thought to herself, I'll tell him some home truths. "Because I asked Mike to make love to me so he carried me through to my bedroom and that is where we spent the night. Now you know!" He was hurt. She didn't need him after all, this was a huge dent in his ego, as he didn't think she would make it without him, but he was proven wrong. "I won't give up on you, I'll be back," he said, as he let himself out.

Lauren went to the sliding doors and opened them and walked out onto the balcony; she needed some fresh sea air. Then she gazed out to the horizon. The sea was calm today, not like yesterday, the waves crashing noisily onto the beach tossing everything in its wake. Was that poor girl out there somewhere? Tears formed in her eyes. She would be so alone, she was someone's daughter, but whose? She was disturbed by the noise of a helicopter as it hovered its way down the coastline. Would the police find anything? "Looks like there must have been sharks spotted out there this morning, I hope the swimmers are safe," called a voice from out of the blue. Lauren was taken by surprise. She looked around to see Mrs Langlands standing out on her balcony. She had never seen her on the balcony, ever! "Yes, they must have spotted some near the shore, to be flying so close in," replied Lauren. With this she walked inside, as she felt vulnerable, just passing words with the Langlands now sent a shiver down her spine. She hoped it would all soon be over and they were locked away.

It was five o'clock and Lauren was starting on reception. She wondered what would transpire later tonight. Who would do the drug drop-off? She hadn't heard from Mike so didn't know what the search had yielded! She was busy catching up on her bookwork and the night went by without much happening. Guests were coming and going but no one stopped to talk. Just before nine o'clock she received a call from Mike. "What we have been looking for has turned up in the next bay, it was washed up on the rocks." He had to be careful when passing classified information over the phone. Lauren thanked him. She felt sick, her worst fears were realised, she had to fight hard to hold back her tears. She couldn't wait to close reception and make her way to her apartment, away from it all.

She was waiting for the lift to come down; it had been up to the sixth floor and was now stopping at the fourth floor. She wondered who would get out on the ground floor. As the door opened, out walked a young girl with a backpack. Surely not, had they recruited another mule to do the drop-offs? Lauren was in total shock, she had to find out! She didn't catch the lift up, she waited until the girl left the building then she took off her high heels and headed down to the beach in her bare feet. She knew where the drop-off point was so she crept down under the cover of the tussocks to where the cross sticks were planted in the sand. Thank goodness it was a moonlit night. Lauren waited and, true to form, the drop-off was made by this new mule who scurried her way back along the beach. Lauren didn't leave, she stayed to see who the recipient was. This time it was a bearded man. He dug up the parcel and put it in his shoulder bag, then he took something from his pocket and buried it. Lauren was terrified; she waited for him to disappear. Would she go down and see what was buried? She stood up, no one was around, so she went to the hot spot. She dug in the sand and found the package, she tried to undo it but it was firmly tied together. On the outside of the package was a loose piece of paper. She would take this off, perhaps it would have some clues. She was taking a big risk but she wanted to find out what was being left once the drop-off was done. She presumed it would be money, payment for the drugs. She had to get out of there, as she remembered the girl would come back and retrieve the buried package. She crept along the dunes until she came to the steps leading to the apartment block.

Just as she was coming up the stairs, towards her came the young girl with her backpack. Lauren felt sick, she certainly didn't want to be recognised. would she be connected to the missing piece of paper that was attached to the package? She put her head down, then realised she still had her uniform on. The girl was just as elusive as Lauren, so hopefully there was no recognition. She hurried into the foyer and caught the lift up to her apartment. As soon as she was inside, she reached for the light switch to see what she had retrieved from the buried parcel. It wasn't money but it was a list of names with amounts of money next to each name. Oh my God, what have I done? thought Lauren. What will happen when they know this is missing? Were they drug debts, did they have another list? Poor Lauren, her mind was all over the place. Would the girl have recognised her? If so, would she tell the Langlands that it was her she saw on the beach late last night? So many questions! What would Mike say, would he be annoyed with her? It was time for a snack and a coffee, as she had not eaten since lunch time.

Today Lauren felt annoyed with herself for having been seen coming from the beach late at night. She had taken a big risk, one that had now perhaps put her in danger. Her mind went back to the bugged apartment. What was coming from there? she wondered. Mike had called, he was on his way to see her to let her know about yesterday's findings. She couldn't erase the memory of the missing girl from her mind, and now a new one, what fate would befall her? She was looking forward to seeing him again, as happy memories surfaced from their wonderful night together. She hoped there would be plenty more! Suddenly there was a knock on her door and in he walked. He came straight over to her and took her in his arms. "How is my little minx today?" he greeted her. "I have missed you, you made me so happy." She just had to let him know the joy he had brought her. "Come and sit down while I tell you what has happened to our missing girl. Adding to our phone conversation from yesterday a body was found washed up on the rocks in the next bay. The police had to retrieve it from the helicopter, as it would have been washed back out to sea with the next tide. At this stage it appears to be our young lady. A postmortem is being carried out at this moment." "Oh Mike, that is so sad. I just want to cry for that young girl, she is someone's daughter. To think the criminals that used her have just brushed her aside, I can't believe there are such people around. But even worse, they have recruited another young girl as their mule." Mike was confused, "What do you mean, how do you know this?"

Lauren told him how she had followed her and saw it all happen. He was angry with her. "Fancy putting yourself in such danger, these people are ruthless, that was stupid, Lauren." He was right, it was stupid of her. She didn't know if she should tell him what she had done next, but it was better to start a relationship without secrets. "Mike, I don't know how to tell you this, but you must know. I waited and witnessed the drop-off and the pick-up. Then when the coast was clear I went and dug up the parcel but it was bound tightly, I couldn't open it, but I did manage to peel off a piece of paper from around it, then buried it again. When I came back here, I had a look and it was a list with names and amounts beside them. "You what, Lauren? I can't believe you did that, what if someone had seen you? You would have been another statistic. Do not ever think you can take on the underworld, they have mercy on no one. We as trained police would not have done that on our own. This has blown me away!" Poor Mike, he was flabbergasted, what more could he say? "Do you think the girl recognised you? What were you wearing?" Lauren hesitated. She was talking to a police officer, so she had to tell the truth. "I was still in my reception uniform and bare feet." He couldn't believe she had been so careless. "This is serious, Lauren, if she remembers you, you are in serious trouble. This is police work, leave it to us to sort out in future. I am really disappointed that you have put yourself in this position. Do you still have the list?" he asked. She went and picked it up and handed it to him. He looked at it to see if he recognised any of the names. One stood out above the rest, thus registering a huge shock. He hid his dismay, there had been enough damage today. The list went into his pocket.

Lauren could see she had upset Mike, so didn't bother

to ask what was going on in apartment nine. All this was better forgotten at the moment. "I'm sorry, Mike, I didn't think of the consequences, it won't happen again," she assured him. Just at that moment a call came through on his cellphone, "Yes, I will come straight away. I'm sorry, Lauren, but I am needed back at the station. I'll call you," and with this he left. She felt sick inside, she had let him down. Is that why he dashed away, was he not interested in her any more? This thought upset her and the tears flowed. She had fallen in love with him, she couldn't lose him now! Was this the end of her new-found happiness?

Reception duties called, so she was back behind the desk, but she wasn't dressed in her uniform, she had hidden it. Tomorrow she would buy Anna and herself new uniforms, the old ones would be destroyed. She didn't feel safe any more, but she only had herself to blame! How could she have been so stupid to have gone down to the beach in her office uniform? As she was scolding herself, she noticed the Langlands leaving the building. This was most unusual for them to be leaving at this time of night. Was this because last night's pick-up package was not complete, was something missing, whose life was in jeopardy now? As soon as 9.30 arrived Lauren locked up reception and hurriedly caught the lift up to the fourth floor. Just as she stepped out, there sitting on the floor outside the Langlands' apartment was the young girl she had seen yesterday. Her eyes were glassy and she was disorientated. Lauren knew she was drugged. "Are you all right?" she asked. "I can't find my way home." "Where is home?" asked Lauren. "I don't know, I can't find the door." With this she helped the girl to her feet and walked her to the door which was unlocked, then took her inside, and sat her in a chair. "Will you be all right? Are you on your own?" She told Lauren they were at a Salvation Army meeting. "Who are they?" she asked. "The Stuarts, Isla and Robert," came back her answer. Lauren asked her how she knew them. "Through the Salvation Army, they help young girls." Now a picture was forming, and it wasn't a pretty one. "I have to go now, are you okay?" asked Lauren, but there was no answer, the girl's lights had gone out, she was away in la-la land. Lauren closed the door and went to her own apartment.

Things were starting to form in Lauren's mind, things that didn't add up. She felt vulnerable, were these poor girls going to the Salvation Army for help to get off drugs? Were they placed with their own members who were meant to supply a safe house for them? Instead the Langlands were exploiting them. That explained why when the last girl disappeared, they did nothing, they just replaced her with someone else's daughter. Their lives amounted to nothing, one life was replaced with another. Not only were the Langlands drug dealers, they exploited young girls. Lauren was shocked. This is what was happening, they were supplying them with drugs to turn them into their drug mules. How disgusting was that?

As she climbed into bed, her thoughts went back to the Langlands' supposed daughter. She was lying in a mortuary, she was someone's daughter and they had no idea what had happened to her. She was alone, in no one's thoughts other than Lauren's. The tears started. Was this going to happen to the new recruit? Would she meet the same fate? No, she would not allow this to happen. Something happened within Lauren, she made a promise to herself that this young girl was going to get a second chance at life. Then she remembered the girl had called the Langlands by a different name. Try as she did to recall the name, it would not come to her. Then she remembered the bug in the apartment — her conversation that took place with the young girl would have been recorded as she put her in a chair. The police would have that information, thank goodness! She cuddled into her pillow wishing it was Mike that she had in her arms; just thinking about him brought on more tears. But did he feel different about her now? She was an irresponsible person!

This morning it was off to a department store to buy new uniforms. The old ones had to be disposed of. She hoped the young girl had forgotten what Lauren was wearing that night and if she never saw them again, then it wouldn't prompt her memory. She would ask Anna to try it on as soon as she arrived back and once on, it could stay on. As she was driving home, she wondered what today would bring. Surely it could only get better! On arrival, she carried the parcels up to reception. "Anna, I have bought us new uniforms for front desk, time for a change. Hop into the office and try it on." Anna looked surprise. "Why do we need a new uniform?" she asked. "Whether we need one or not doesn't matter, we are having one." With this Anna disappeared into the office and came out with a totally new look. "That's great, more modern, leave it on it is now our official uniform." "What is wrong with you, Lauren, why the change?" she asked. "I'm the boss, don't ask questions," and with this she gave her the other parcel with the second uniform, then she left and caught the lift up to the fourth floor. Anna was baffled by Lauren's irrational behaviour. Was it because of this guy Mike, had he distracted her thinking pattern, was she in love?

Lauren waited all day to hear from Mike but with no results. She was still angry with herself. Had she lost him?

Then she was disturbed by a phone call. "Lauren, a very large parcel has arrived for apartment twelve, I just thought I would let you know. The Langlands must do online selling with the amount of deliveries they get." Lauren agreed. If only she knew, but it was too soon to tell her what was happening, it was still a confidential police matter. Time for her reception duty, so she caught the lift. It stopped at the third floor and in got one of the detectives. He spoke to Lauren and she asked him how many men stayed on call at night. He told her only one at night and that was Lance, but there were two shifts during the day, because not a lot happened at night. She was happy to know this, as they would have recorded the conversation between her and the young girl, so the true name of the Langlands, known to the Salvation Army, would be on tape as well as other vital information. When Lauren saw the size of the package that had been delivered today, it was the largest one yet. Thoughts started running through her mind. How was the young girl going to manage it? Surely it must be several nights' drop-offs! Just at that moment, Mr Langlands arrived to pick up his package. "Hi, girls, new uniform, I like it," he said. "See, Anna, someone appreciates our new uniform," joked Lauren.

The night shift was coming to an end and Lauren felt a little down; she still hadn't heard from Mike. She locked up reception then went to the foyer door, only to catch sight of the young girl struggling along the path with the large parcel. Where was she taking this? It couldn't be buried, but then she wasn't heading to the beach. Lauren watched with interest. The girl walked along the path then down towards the basement carpark. She put the parcel down and fumbled with her key trying to unlock the garage door. When it automatically went up, she picked up the parcel and struggled to a nearby car. She checked the number plate and sat the parcel in front of the car. Then she rang someone on her phone. By this time Lauren had decided to run back to the foyer to see which floor the lift was coming from. The girl had definitely rung someone in the building, as the car must have belonged to a guest, otherwise it would not have been parked in there. The lift stopped at the third floor and picked someone up then continued down to the basement carpark. She didn't know who was staying on the third floor, only the police surveillance guy. She would wait and once the lift was on its way up, she would press the button and it would stop and pick her up. She didn't have to wait long and was surprised that when the door opened, there was the night detective. Why was he there? He must have just driven into the carpark. Damn, had she botched up again? Then who did that car belong to that the parcel was left at? Once the police guy was dropped off at the third floor and the lift made its way up to the fourth floor, Lauren decided not to get out but backtracked back to the basement. By the time she arrived the parcel was gone. It must have been picked up, but by who? Perhaps it was nothing to do with the car it was placed by?

A disappointed Lauren made her way to her apartment. She had a chance, and had missed it. But why did the girl not go straight down in the lift to the basement carpark instead of leaving the building and entering by the outside entrance? It didn't make sense, but if she was on drugs, she wouldn't be thinking logically. Lauren would check the car number-plate tomorrow. All she wanted to do was fall into bed, as she felt exhausted and disappointed. Please, please ring me, Mike, she pleaded, but no call came through.

The first job on Lauren's list this morning was to go

to the basement and get the number-plate of the car the parcel was left by. But when she got there it was gone, the park was empty! How stupid of me, why didn't I do it last night? she scolded herself. She was falling to pieces, here was another missed opportunity. This was a vital one. Damn, she muttered to herself. After catching the lift back to her apartment, she opened the glass sliding doors and walked out onto the balcony. She needed some fresh air. She stood and looked up the beach. It was a beautiful day and the waves were breaking gently on the sand. In the distance she could see a lonely figure staggering along the beach. Was that the girl from apartment twelve? It certainly looked like her, but she never went out during the day. Lauren watched her disappearing among the sand dunes. Was this another opportunity to meet up with her again? She hurried to the lift and caught it down to the basement and let herself out the side door. This way she didn't have to speak with Anna; it would save her time. She took the path onto the street and hurried along a couple of blocks then went down onto the sand dunes. By doing this, no peering eyes from the apartment block would see her.

She searched along the dunes and it wasn't long before she came across the girl curled up in a foetal position among the long grasses. Lauren watched her closely — she seemed to be having fits or seizures, her body was moving violently. Lauren thought this must be the effects of the drugs she was taking, or perhaps she had overdosed. This thought frightened her. What if something happened to her? She was alone. She went over and sat beside her. The young girl's body was now quivering, so Lauren reached out and took her hand. She felt the girl grasp on to her, so she moved closer and put her arms around her. "Is that you, mother?" the girl sobbed as she clung to Lauren. The sobs got louder. "I'm sorry, so sorry," she kept muttering over and over again. "It's all right, I'm here with you, you are not alone," she told the young girl. With this comforting thought she drifted off into her own messed-up world.

Lauren sat with her for nearly two hours before there was any response. When she eventually opened her eyes her pupils were dilated, she was still under the influence of drugs. "Where am I?" she asked. Lauren explained that she had come across her lying in the sand, while out walking. "Do you know me?" "I have seen you a couple of times at the apartments," Lauren told her. The girl hesitated. "But I don't know you." Lauren realised then that the drugs were affecting her ability to think clearly, in fact they had messed with her brain. "What do you do?" asked Lauren. "I work for people." "Do you get paid?" she asked. "I don't get money, they give me free drugs so I don't need money," she answered. "Why are you using drugs? They aren't good for you," Lauren tried to point out to her. "I know but I can't get away from them. I went to the Salvation Army for help, they gave me to people who were meant to foster me, but it hasn't worked." "What if I could get you help, would you leave these people?" Lauren asked. "I can't, they would find me and hurt me, the other man told me this, when he was hurting me. I am not allowed to talk." So, these were the tactics the dealers used over these young girls. What did she mean by the other man, was that the Asian?

Then Lauren's thoughts drifted back to the supposed daughter and how her life had ended. Her only way to escape this horrible wasted life was to walked into the sea. Perhaps she did this on purpose to escape all the abuse, perhaps she didn't overdose. This was still haunting her, and now another young life hung in the balance. "What is your name?" Lauren asked. "I think it is Sally McIntyre, I can't remember much, something about Lismore. I will have to go back now, I might have another burial to do." Lauren almost found this funny, but it was no laughing matter. At last she had a lead, she would try to find this young girl's family, as she needed help immediately. As she got up, the young girl took Lauren's hand. "You are a nice lady, I won't tell anyone I know you," she whispered. Then she walked away. Lauren stood and watched her making her way back down the beach to the apartments. She was much steadier on her feet now. What a terrible effect the drugs had on her. Lauren had never seen this reaction before, but then she had never been around drugs or druggies, so this was all new to her. She hated what she saw of the drug scene. Ruthless dealers preying on the vulnerable, how wrong was that?

As Lauren was passing reception, Anna called out to her. "You had a visitor, guess who?" "Don't tell me it was Scott?" "No, it was Mike, he was looking for you. I rang but you didn't answer, so he left." "Bugger, did he leave a message?" asked Lauren. "He said he would call back later." This cheered her up, he hadn't forgotten her after all! First thing on her mind at the moment was to go to the White Pages on the computer and add McIntyre, Lismore, to see what appeared. Yes, it did yield results, ten to be exact! Where would she start? There was only one way to tackle this and that was to start at the top of the page. All she could do was ask if they knew of a young girl named Sally. Lauren got on to this straight away; she wanted it all sorted before she started on reception.

Two more names were left on the list, then it was back to square one! She rang the second last number. A lady answered. "Hello, I'm Lauren. I was wondering if you know of a young girl named Sally McIntyre?" "Why do you ask?" "Because she is in need of urgent help. I'm trying to contact her family. Can you help me, please?" she asked. "Sally is my daughter, I haven't heard from her for two years. She went off the rails, we don't know where she is." This didn't take Lauren by surprise. "She is very sick, she is on drugs and is working as a drug mule for dealers. She wants to get out, but is petrified of retribution. Can you help her, can she come home?" Lauren asked. There was a pause on the end of the phone. "Her father and I have parted. I have a new partner, I'd have to talk to him first before I can give you an answer," she said. "Please help her, the last young girl took her own life, it was the only way she could escape this cruel existence. We have to get Sally out before it is too late!" pleaded Lauren. "I will leave my number, please ring me as soon as possible?" She heard a faint 'Thank you' then the lady hung up. My God, what is wrong with parents today? she wondered. But not having been part of the drug scene, she had no idea of the heartache this brought to a family, and how cruel the rehabilitation process was to everyone around that person. One merely existed from one day to the next, while trying to get by, thinking about the next fix, which was not going to be forthcoming. The highs and lows, it was a nightmare for all concerned. The supporters suffered as deeply as the person going through the withdrawal period. It was a long, drawn-out process!

The phone brought Lauren to heel. What was the time? She got the shock of her life. She was meant to be in reception. "Hello, Lauren, did you want me to stay on for a bit?" asked Anna. "Gosh, I'm sorry, I'll be down in a tick, time has run away on me," and with this she hung up and did a quick change. So much had happened in the last two days, she felt lost, lost to herself and lost to the world around her. Such sadness had surrounded her, not what she had expected to come with her new job. But this was the nature of this bustling area; there were highs and lows but unfortunately more lows than highs seemed to be coming her way! She had never realised how vulnerable life was, for young girls who had lost their way. They were easy prey for predators, who were always waiting in the wings to pounce, and have their dirty work done for drugs, not money. It was happening right here in her own apartment block. How she longed to be in Mike's arms, feeling his strong heart beating against her soft skin, then all this would disappear even for a few wonderful moments!

Just as Lauren turned her back to lock up, she felt arms encasing her. She didn't have to turn around to know who these belonged to. Right here was the man she thought she had lost. "Hi, I've been away on an undercover assignment so wasn't able to contact you until it was over. Now I have three days off, so be prepared." "Be prepared for what?" she asked him with a cheeky grin. "For whatever comes next, my little minx." They caught the lift up to her apartment. Lauren wanted to know if there were any more reports on the drowned girl. "Did the postmortem find anything on her?" she asked. "There were scars on her upper back and her buttocks, but this was not the cause of her death. They have ruled out foul play, but there were drugs in her system, so it was classified as a drug overdose." "What happened to her body?" "It is still in the mortuary, no one has claimed it. The police are still making enquiries," he told her. Lauren voiced her opinion: "That is so sad. Why does this happen? She is someone's daughter, for God's sake, what would they be thinking if they knew this was where she was? I hate the drug scene, it is an underworld of deceit and lies." "I know, Lauren, but sadly it is not going to go away. People are becoming greedier and at any cost. Money speaks all languages, and sadly this is the quickest way to make a buck, so it will always be an ongoing problem. We in the police force do our best to try to combat it, but we will never win over drugs. The dealers are tight-lipped people who work in the seedy underworld and some use charities as cover-ups, as well you know, you have it going on right here." Then Lauren asked Mike what had been uncovered from the bugged apartment. He told her they were still building a case, the evidence had to be convincing when taken to court, there could be no loopholes for the dealers' defence to tear apart. She wondered if she should tell him about the new recruit. No, it could wait until tomorrow, there were more pressing things on her mind!

They opened a bottle of wine and went out on the balcony as it was a balmy night. A sea breeze took away some of the humidity leaving it very pleasant. They stood together and Mike put his arms around her so he could feel her close to him, he had missed her. "I thought I had lost you because of my daft detective work," she told him. "I was angry not because of what you did, but for the dangerous position you put yourself in. You cannot mess with these guys, they are ruthless and have no pity for anyone. They will even kill their own to get what they want and where they want to go. Stay away from them, Lauren, it is not a pretty world out there," Mike advised her. As they were moving from the balcony to go inside, Lauren spotted the young girl on her balcony. She looked at Lauren and moved her hand in front of her and gave her a secret wave. Did she remember Lauren from this morning, that she had told her she was a nice lady? Whether this was a good thing or not, she wasn't sure; as long as she didn't mention her to the Langlands. She would tell Mike about it tomorrow.

"I presume you are staying the night with me?" she asked. "If I'm allowed, then the answer is yes." Lauren went up to him and kissed him passionately. "I'm going to take a quick shower, shan't be long," then she disappeared. She undressed and stood under the shower letting the water cascade down her body. She closed her eyes thinking of what lay ahead. Suddenly she felt hands caressing her wet body starting at her shoulders and working their way down to her lower body. She turned around to face Mike, she lathered his body, teasing him, touching his manly parts then cheekily pinching his buttocks. It was too much, he couldn't restrain himself any longer. He pulled Lauren hard against his body and she felt his hands reaching under her buttocks and gently lifting her, leaning her against the shower wall so he could take her. This was something she had never experienced before, making love in the shower, but why, it was fun! The shower was Scott's sacred place, he wouldn't share it with anyone, he was in control at all times. Get out of my head, she said to herself. Why had it not happened before? At twenty-seven, a girl was meant to have experienced all these things.

She had met Scott when she was seventeen; she was the receptionist for him and his wife at their resort. Then the affair started and once she was caught up in it, she couldn't get out. At first it was fun, it was flattering to be admired by an older man, a man of standing ... her boss. But as the relationship progressed, cracks started to appear. Scott started controlling her every movement, and then when the wife found out, she offered Lauren some advice. "You are ruining your life. I was you once, and after you there will be someone else." At the time she thought this was the jealous wife trying to frighten her away, but she found out too late, how true those words were. It took ten years for it to happen, but eventually it did. She handed the same advice on to the next victim and she, like Lauren, didn't listen. But Lucy was smart, she didn't hang around, now he decided he wanted Lauren back! Mike was different, he made her feel good about herself, there were no restrictions, and to make love in the shower, how innovative! He thought outside the square, that was what was exciting about him, and they both shared the same passion for helping the vulnerable young. Other than that, all she knew was that he was single and an undercover detective, nothing else mattered at the moment.

Lauren woke this morning with happiness in her heart. Mike was lying beside her sound asleep. She didn't want to disturb him so climbed out of bed, dressed and went into the dining room. Just as she was putting the jug on, there was a quiet tapping on her door. As she opened it, the young girl from next door pushed past her, in a rush to get inside. "They have gone out, I've had my drugs, please hold my hand?" she pleaded to Lauren. She grabbed Lauren's hand and held on to it tightly. Lauren was shocked, what should she do? But the girl was having a seizure. Her eyes were rolling and she was shaking violently. Lauren led her to the settee and lay her down, all the time holding her hand. Had she come to Lauren for help, was this what happened each time she was fed drugs? It had happened yesterday and now today! Was she being used as a guinea pig to trial different drugs? She felt sick, what bastards would do this to a young defenceless girl? She had to get her away from the Langlands, but how?

Mike had just woken up and walked out to the lounge. "What is happening?" he asked, as he saw the settee occupied. Then when another seizure came on, Mike knew what going on, as he had seen it dozens of times. "Who is she?" "This is the Langlands' new recruit," she told him. "You are joking, she is but a child. What is she doing here?" Now it was time to start right at the beginning and tell him everything. How she first found her slumped in the hallway outside apartment twelve, and she had no idea where she was so she took her into her apartment. She was asking for her mother. "Mike, it was so sad, I had to leave her there so as not to be seen by the Langlands. Then yesterday I saw her staggering along the beach and disappear into the sand dunes." The tears were running down her cheeks as she relayed it all to him and how she had sat with her for two hours, waiting for the drugs to wear off. She felt it was her duty to be there for her. "But how did she get tied up with the Langlands?" he asked. "She went to the Salvation Army for help and they placed her with them, thinking she was going to a safe place of refuge, where she would be fostered and nurtured. The Salvation Army are probably oblivious to what is really going on, because the Langlands are regular churchgoers, they attend every Sunday." Mike was shocked. "Where does this leave you, Lauren? If she talks to them about you, what then?" "She is my only friend, no one knows I have a friend," whispered a little voice from the settee. They both looked at her, her eyes were starting to focus and tears were forming. "No one knows, promise," she sobbed. Lauren sat beside her and held her in her arms. The shaking had stopped, she was coming back to the real world. "I am here for you, Sally, but we must get you back before the Langlands come home. I promise I will get you out of here soon." Lauren had made a promise that she fully intended to honour. Mike checked to see that no one was coming up in the lift, then Lauren walked Sally back to her apartment, still a little unsteady on her feet. Lauren opened the door, gave her a big hug and ran back along the hallway so as not to be seen. Once safely in her apartment she burst into tears, she was devastated. How much longer did that poor girl have to suffer? She told Mike among her tears, "I have rung her mother and told her Sally needed help and I'm still waiting for a reply! How could people do this to their children?" "Lauren, you have not seen what real life is like out there, it can be a cruel world. Some parents are solo, they have no money and no support, so they just give up on their children. They can barely care for themselves. I have seen it all and it is far from pretty, in fact it can be downright ugly."

# 4

# A planned rescue

Where had the time gone? Mike was due back at work today. Last night had been a long one. Most of the hours were not wasted, spent in ardent workouts between the sheets. They were both in need of an early night away from each other tonight! Lauren had still not heard back from Sally's mother, so she picked up the phone. "Hello, Mrs McIntyre, it's Lauren, I have been waiting to hear back from you, about your daughter Sally?" "I'm sorry but I lost your number and didn't know how to contact you. We have talked it over and yes, she can come back, we can only but try," she said. "It won't be easy as she is still on drugs, but she wants to give them up, so this is a positive start. Can we bring her down?" asked Lauren. "Yes, but give us a week, then call when you are leaving," she told her. This gave Lauren a timetable to work to. Hopefully the police would be finished with their investigation and the Langlands would be out of the picture and locked up for a very long time.

Tonight, as Lauren was locking up, she saw the lift stop

at the fourth floor. Was this going to be Sally doing a drug drop-off? She waited but the lift went straight to the basement carpark. That is strange, she thought, so she left the building and walked down the path to the carpark. She took her master key out of her pocket and quietly opened the side door. As she crept in, she saw the detective Lance locking up his car. Lauren watched as he caught the lift back, then she had a peep in his car and sitting on the front passenger's seat was a parcel. She tried to make sense of all this, but the lift had come from the fourth floor and he was based on the third floor. What would he be doing on that floor? Then suddenly, Lauren realised this was the same car that the parcel was placed by the other night. This must be the detective's car! Oh my God, she thought, no, that couldn't be right. Was he mixed up in the drug scene with the Langlands, a cop? No way. There must another simple explanation, but try as she did, she couldn't find one. A crooked cop, was there such a thing? What would he want drugs for? He wouldn't be taking them, not while in the police force, someone would notice, surely? The only other reason would be to make money. If this was so, he was a lowlife just like the Langlands. Would Mike know about this? How would she discuss it with him?

Only two days to go before Lauren got Sally away from the Langlands. She had arranged for Anna to work two shifts, so she could drive Sally back to Lismore. It would take a full day and half the night to get there and back. She saw Sally leaving the building with her backpack to do a burial, as she called it. Hopefully this would be her final delivery. The police had arranged a meeting with Lauren on the Monday, the day after she had taken Sally home. The Langlands would leave for the Salvation Army church service on Sunday morning, and this was when Lauren would go to their apartment and get Sally out. This had not been discussed with Sally, as Lauren was frightened she would let something slip while under the influence of drugs. She could not risk this!

Lauren was happy to know that tomorrow she would free Sally from the terrible existence she was living. Mike couldn't come as he was on another undercover assignment. She tossed and turned all night, planning the getaway. She would ring Sally's mother as she was about to leave, as promised.

Today was the day when it was all going to happen! Lauren showered and put on a sweater and some jeans. She rang down to Anna to see if the Langlands had left for church, but she hadn't seen them leave as yet. "Ring me as soon as they come down," she instructed. She waited by the phone. Half an hour went by, then an hour, by this time Lauren was starting to panic! She made her way to apartment nine on the third floor where the police surveillance was being conducted. She knocked on the door and was asked to come in. "Can you tell me if there are any movements happening in the above apartment?" she asked. "Actually, when Lance left, he said the only thing he heard all night was a muffled cry in the early hours of the morning, but nothing since." Lauren's heart missed a beat and a shiver went down her spine. Did that cry belong to Sally? What had they done to her? "Come, we must go to the apartment and see what has happened," said an anxious Lauren. "But the investigation isn't finished yet, we are not at liberty to break protocol," he replied. "Something has happened, I'm going to see," and with this she left. The detective wasn't far behind her.

Lauren ran up the stairs and unlocked the apartment door with her master key. It was empty, all their personal belongings were gone. They must have done a runner during the night, but what of Sally? The detective was shocked. That is why there had been no movements recorded, but why didn't Lance pick this up on his shift? Perhaps he was tired. Lauren felt sick. She had made a promise to Sally that she would take her away from all this, now it had been broken. She broke down and cried, she felt powerless, but no way would she let this beat her. She would find her, this promise she had made to herself and to Sally, it was going to be kept, at any cost! "I'm sorry but I just came on duty at seven o'clock so I don't know the whole story, other than what Lance had mentioned. Something about a muffled cry but he just dismissed it as it didn't persist. It looks like they have absconded," the detective said. "Would there not have been something on the device to indicate they were leaving, surely they would have talked about it?" asked Lauren. She was devastated. Tomorrow was her meeting at the police station, she would demand some answers!

The detective left to report back to the station on what had happened. Lauren sat and cried a river of tears. She had broken a promise to someone who needed help, a defenceless druggie, who was now shifted to another address, to continue pushing drugs for the Langlands. She got up and searched the apartment from top to bottom, hoping to find a clue as to where they might have gone, but the search yielded nothing. What next? Then she remembered a little advice Mike had offered her, that drug dealers were professionals at their own game and sometimes they outsmarted the police. Here was the reminder! All that was left to do now was ring Sally's mother to say she wouldn't be bringing her home. She wondered if she would be sad or relieved.

Now it was time to let Anna in on what was happening. The only reason Lauren hadn't told her was because she didn't want her to worry or be caught up in any reprisals that may have occurred if it had all turned to custard. She made her way to reception. The check-outs were finished, so now was the time, before the new arrivals started coming in. After listening to all Lauren had to say, Anna was shocked. She was mystified at all the parcels the Langlands received and, as she had mentioned, thought they were involved in online selling, when all the time they were dealing in drugs. But what saddened her most, like Lauren, was the plight of the poor girls. After hearing it all, Anna could see that Lauren was badly cut up, so told her she would still work the double shift as organised and for Lauren to take the rest of the day off. Lauren was grateful for this, as she still needed time to think things over.

Back in her apartment, Lauren had the dreaded job of calling Sally's mother to let her know what had happened, that she wouldn't be coming home. She picked up the phone and called, but there was no answer, so she left a message on the answerphone for her to ring Lauren as soon as possible. Now it was time to jot down in a notebook all the dates when certain things happened that were relevant to that time. One of the main things was the Langlands' other name, as mentioned by Sally. It had slipped Lauren's mind and try as she did, she could not recall it, it was gone. But thank God it would be on the listening device. As soon as she had the name, she would go to the Salvation Army and start some enquiries. This gave her heart, it was what kept her going at the moment. At tomorrow's meeting with the police, all would be revealed. It was just a matter of surviving until then!

# 5

# What happened to the evidence?

Lauren walked into the police station armed with her notebook and pen. She was going to find out all the information she needed. She was shown to the room with the boardroom table, where some of the undercover drug squad members were seated. The police superintendent told everyone present they had gone through the listening devices and they yielded very little information. He couldn't understand why this had happened. There were little snippets here and there, but nothing much in the way of incriminating evidence. The one thing that was recorded was the phone calls from reception to say there were parcels for them to pick up. This in itself pointed to something sinister going on, but circumstantial evidence was what was needed. Lauren requested that the recording on the night of the 17th be replayed. The tape was fast forwarded to the night shift. There was general conversation then Mrs Langlands told Sally they were going to a Salvation Army meeting and she was not to leave the apartment. There was a treat for her on the bench for being a good girl. Then there was a noise and the door closed. Then silence reigned. The next words spoken were from the Langlands when they arrived home from the meeting.

But wait a minute, where was the conversation between her and Sally? Lauren had brought her in from the hallway and she had told her the names of the people she was working for and it wasn't Langlands. Also, that she was placed with them from the Salvation Army. Where was all this information? "Stop this here for a minute?" asked Lauren. "Who was the detective on that night?" "It is recorded here as officer Lance. Why do you want to know this for?" enquired the superintendent. Lauren was in shock, she didn't know what to do. She didn't want to tread on any corns before she had spoken with Mike. "It's okay, thank you."

It was another day before Mike contacted Lauren. He was away on another undercover placement, which had taken him out of town. "Hi, Lauren, I'm back, can I come around later? I've got a couple of days off." "Mike, I need to talk to you, it's urgent. Yes, come as soon as possible, please!" she pleaded. But of course, she was in reception until 9.30pm, so it would have to be after that. The night went by slowly, as she wished for it to get a move on. Why did this always happen when one was in a hurry? she asked herself. It wasn't as if it had never happened before. Was there a reason for this? Did it happen to give a person time to think things over, before they rushed into something that needed a bit more thought? There were plenty of things going on in her head. How was she going to tell Mike she thought, no, knew, a colleague was in the drug scene with the Langlands? Yes, she definitely needed time to think this over!

Closing time had finally arrived. Lauren locked up reception, then checked to see if Mike was there, but he wasn't, so she caught the lift up to her apartment. She felt a little down, so decided to have a quick shower and change into something more comfortable. By the time Mike arrived, she was nestled into her favourite chair sipping a wine, wondering how she was going to approach the subject of Lance. She had filled two glasses. "Hi, my little minx, have you missed me?" Lauren smiled. She didn't have to say anything, her smile said it all. "What is so important that you want to discuss with me?" he asked. All her thinking time had not prepared her for this! Where would she start? Her heart started beating a little faster. Just do it, she told herself.

"I had a meeting with your colleagues at the station, but pieces of the voice recording were missing." "What do you mean, Lauren?" he asked. She told him about the night she took Sally back into her apartment and how she had given out information, but it was not recorded on the tape. "Can pieces be erased?" she asked. "No, I don't think so, but it can be turned off so it doesn't record. Who was on that night, do you know?" "Yes, it was a guy named Lance." Lauren watched Mike's reactions. She didn't know how he would feel if she was to accuse him of dishonesty. "I think he is mixed up with the Langlands." "What makes you say that?" he questioned her. Lauren told him about the parcels delivered to the basement carpark and that she had seen him putting one in his vehicle, one that Sally had dropped off. Lauren was nervous. Would this be the end of their relationship, was it all worth informing on his colleague? More to the point, would he believe her?

Mike looked at Lauren, thinking to himself that she was one smart cookie. "Lauren, this is classified information I am going to give you, but I know I can trust you. Remember that list you gave me, the one you so bravely dug up that night? Lance's named was on it, as a debtor. With what you have just told me, yes, he is definitely dealing in drugs. I didn't want to believe it at the start, he is a drug squad colleague of mine, but this will have to be investigated." "I am so angry, Mike, as I now don't have the names the Langlands go under when they deal with the Salvation Army. I have no leads, I must find Sally, it is driving me crazy. I think about her all the time, and the promise I made to her," sobbed Lauren. "I can help you, I will put Lance under police surveillance, as he will still be dealing with them. We will find their new location then we will rescue Sally. This cheered Lauren up a little. She was not in the habit of making promises that she could not keep, her word was her honour. "What will happen to your colleague?" she asked. "Don't worry about him, he will be dealt with. This is a serious breach of police conduct, especially as he is part of the drug squad. He has gone against what he stands for. What a rat!" Lauren felt a little more at ease, there was still hope on the horizon for her to find Sally.

"Let's forget police business, that's not what I came for. I came for business of another kind, one that just involves you and me," teased Mike. "What about monkey business, does that sound better?" "Right, monkey business it is!" They cuddled up on the settee and finished their bottle of wine. Thank goodness that was all sorted. Now she felt relaxed, so jumped up and led him through to her bedroom. Now the monkey business was about to begin. They raced to see who undressed and was in bed first. Of course it was Mike, as he had less clothes to shed. This was male dominance! But Lauren didn't complain, God knows she had waited for this night. Just to feel Mike's hands roaming her body brought on warm, tingling feelings. Then there was no stopping once this happened, she lost all control of responsibility, and became the irresponsible minx that he had named her. He had become a big part of her life, in fact the first male she felt completely relaxed with. They both liked to tease each other, which in turn brought on laughter and that is what made this relationship so special.

When Mike woke up this morning, he left Lauren sleeping. He dressed and left the apartment, as he had business to attend to at the police station. First, he had to talk with his superior about Lance being mixed up in drug dealing. This would not go down well, no one in the force liked a crooked cop for a colleague. But a drug squad member, this was not on. His job was to combat against drugs, not sell them! Mike's boss was shocked on hearing these allegations, but he didn't doubt Mike. He agreed to put Lance's car under police surveillance, as they had to find the Langlands. They had been beaten by these crooks, which wasn't a good look for the police, in fact it was a cocked-up job by one of their own guys, who was an informant. The police now had enough evidence on the Langlands, but first they would have to locate them. All the evidence in the world was no good if they had no one to charge! While Lance was on the night shift, he would be under surveillance. He would definitely know where they had relocated to, after tipping them off about their apartment being bugged. This was now proven by Lauren, knowing for a fact that a lot of the night happenings were not being recorded. She had dates and times to prove this. This must have been when most of the drug dealings were talked about.

Lauren woke to find Mike gone. She didn't need to guess where he had gone and what he was up to. After last night's talk, lots of secrets had been traded. She thought this morning she would visit the local Salvation Army thrift shop and have a nosy. Perhaps she could talk to someone about troubled young girls going there to find help. This would all be new to her, as she had never visited one of their shops or attended any of their church services. Lauren knew they did good for all communities, and they were a well-respected worldwide organisation. She left a message with Anna for Mike, to let him know she would be back soon, just to make himself at home. She drove to their headquarters where one of their main shops was based. People were coming and going, it certainly was a busy place. Lauren walked through the door and was amazed at the amount and variety of clothes, household items, bedding, everything really. She had not expected this! She browsed through the clothing racks and could see how Mrs Langlands always dressed so nice — some of the clothes looked brand new and were very modern. Not what she expected! As she was browsing, she noticed a lady in a Salvation Army uniform hovering in the background. Perhaps she might be able to shed some light on the placement of wayward girls.

Lauren introduced herself and talked about the shop, trying to soften the atmosphere between them. She told the lady she was thinking of setting up a home for troubled teenage girls, was there an opening, did many young girls come to them looking for help? The answer came back as a definite yes. They did make occasional placements with respectable members of their church who they knew would nurture the girls. Most were regular churchgoers who attended church every Sunday. Lauren nearly flinched when she heard this. She asked the lady her name so she could speak to her again. She then thanked her and said she would be in touch. Now she felt she had achieved something. This was all she could do at the moment, until the Langlands were located, then she could move forward and meet with them again, but with news they would not want to hear!

On her arrival home, Lauren found Mike sitting in a deckchair on the balcony reading a book. "You old sneak, fancy leaving me in bed on my own. Why didn't you wake me?" she asked. "You looked so peaceful and I was on a mission. As from today Lance is under police surveillance, so hopefully he will make his move within the next couple of days, then it will be all go. Not only will the Langlands' life be over, so will his. The rest of the drug squad will be devastated when this all comes out, as we are a closeknit unit. To think he messed up all the other guys' good surveillance work, they will want revenge. What a stupid guy, but he will be his own undoing," stated Mike. Lauren made some sandwiches and brought them out to the balcony, where they had lunch. The sea breeze had edged its way towards the building, thus keeping the heat to a bearable temperature. As Lauren relaxed, she thought back to what she had told the Salvation Army lady. Would she really like to run a home for troubled girls, keeping them out of the hands of predators who used and abused them? With this her thoughts drifted back to Sally and how the drugs had affected her, bringing on seizures. To be there with her and to be able to hold her until it was all over had deeply moved her. Is this my calling? she asked herself. She had lost her heart to these two girls. It was too late for one, but the other must be saved. Hopefully Sally would be rescued before anything happened to her!

Lauren heard her phone ringing so went to answer it. "Lauren, have you heard anything about Sally yet? I just wanted to tell you that she can't come home. My partner's youngest son has been sent to him from his mother, as she can't control him, and he doesn't want a druggie living with us, I'm sorry," she said. "No, we haven't found her yet, but that is sad she can't come home. How do you think she will feel when I tell her this?" "I'm sorry but I have no say, I am living in his house so I can't make any decisions," and with this she hung up. Lauren thought she detected sobs in her voice for having to turn down her daughter's plea for help, but this was her choice, to live with her partner in a relationship where she had no say, or care for her daughter. The choice had been made. Then when she thought back to her life with Scott, it wasn't that much different — she lived in his apartment without any say!

She looked at Mike and was so grateful to have him here with her. She stood up and took his book off him and lured him into her bedroom. She unbuttoned his shirt and slipped it off his shoulders, then turned him around and massaged his neck and shoulders then moved down his body. She pressed on his pressure points in the small of his back, inflicting a pleasurable pain that made him flinch. He had a strong muscular body, but that was the physique needed in his job. Unbeknown to Lauren he had undone his belt and let his shorts fall to the floor. She cheekily pinched his buttocks, then it was all on! She hurriedly slipped off her knickers and jumped on the bed with him where they consummated their love for each other. Satisfaction took over and they both dropped off to sleep. Lauren was woken by the phone, it was Anna wanting to know if she was coming to work. "I'll be down in a minute." Then she looked at the time, it was 5.30, she was half an hour late. It was a quick shower and a quick good-bye, then out the door she flew. "I'm sorry, Lauren, I would have left you two, but I have a prior engagement," said an apologetic Anna. "It's fine, we were just resting." "Pull the other leg," smiled Anna, and they both laughed.

While Lauren was on reception she heard a little cough and looked up to see Scott standing there. "Hi, Lauren, how is it all going?" "I'm fine, how's everything with you?" she enquired. "Well, not so good. I'm having trouble buying into resort management here on the Gold Coast. There are not many properties changing hands, no one seems to want to sell," he said in a disappointed voice. "Well, really, who could blame them, everyone wants to live here, this is meant to be paradise!" Although, at the moment her thoughts were still hovering around a home to rehabilitate young girls troubled with drug addiction. She seemed to have lost her zest for apartment management, it wasn't making her happy any more, she didn't feel fulfilled. Her thoughts were taking her down another path, one that she felt would be helping society and bring hope to those daughters that belonged to someone, but had lost their way. If only she could reunite them with their parents again and become part of the family that they had left. None of this had entered her head before she saw the need with her own eyes. As she thought about this, tears filled her eyes. "Are you okay?" asked Scott. "Oh, I'm sorry, just one of those moments! Scott, if I was thinking of selling my management rights here, would you be interested?" "Really, Lauren? I would love this building!" She told him she would put some more thought into it and if he came back in a week's time, she would have made up her mind. Lauren had made no mention of this to Mike, it was a spur of the moment thought, voiced out loud to Scott.

Mike was back at work, the three love-filled days were over and life was back to normal at the apartments. But Lauren was feeling far from normal. She couldn't get it out of her head that she wanted to help these lost girls. It had consumed her thinking, blocking everything else from entering. She couldn't let go of the young girl lying in the mortuary; no one had claimed her body. She was lost to the world and would be buried as a lost soul, she was alone, but she was still someone's daughter! This haunted Lauren and she worried sick for Sally. What was going to happen to her? Her mother couldn't have her at home. Where was she going to go? She had nowhere. She needed to be loved and nurtured back to a life of acceptance, one that would make her happy again. But how was this going to happen when no one wanted her? With this thought she contacted a real estate agent and asked if he had any four-bedroom homes on his books. This was it, she had started the ball rolling. If she could rescue and look after three young girls at any one time, she would feel she was contributing to making the world a better place, a safer place, for those lost souls that were being abused.

# 6

# Finding the right home

Two days later she has seen five four-bedroom homes and one in particular felt right. Its location was beachfront with a large private back yard, surrounded by shrubs. The front yard was lawn, then a fence separated it from the beach. Lauren had asked Mike to come and view it, as she wanted his opinion. She would tell him what she was thinking while they were standing on the property. She waited anxiously for him to arrive. What would he think? As he walked up to her, she took his hand and they walked around the property. "What do you think?" she asked. "It is big for one person, are you thinking of filling it with little ones?" he joked. "Why four bedrooms?" It was then that Lauren explained to him what she wanted to do, no, what her heart was telling her to do. She felt this was her calling. "I hope, Lauren, you know what you are doing. It isn't going to be easy, but I know how you are feeling. If that is what you want to do, go for it." Lauren hugged him, she knew he would understand. "I have to have somewhere for Sally to live, hopefully it will be soon!"

Mike had some good news for Lauren: "We think we have found the Langlands' new location. Lance visited there last night. Would you believe it is only six blocks from here? We want you to come to the police station tomorrow morning and we will take you to the resort so you can formally identify them. They have changed their names again." "Is Sally still with them?" was Lauren's first question. "We don't know, but we will find out tomorrow." "Oh Mike, that is such good news." She was so excited.

The next morning Anna was on the phone. "I have Scott here at reception." "Please send him up, Anna." When she heard him knock, she unlocked the door. They exchanged pleasantries. "Sorry, Scott, I have only got a few minutes as I have to leave for an appointment. I have decided to sell, so it is yours if you are happy to pay my asking price. She told him what she wanted and he accepted, there and then. "There is only one stipulation: don't mess with Anna. She is a nice young lady, I will not have her hurt!" "Come, Lauren, that's unfair!" he bit back. "I mean it, Scott, don't touch her!" He knew when she meant business and this was one of these times. He agreed to her terms.

Lauren was on her way to the police station to meet up with Mike. She was nervous. How was she going to identify them, surely not face to face? She didn't want them to hunt her down! Suddenly she had arrived. An undercover police car was parked outside the station entrance and Mike was standing with the door open, waiting for her. He was accompanied by a colleague and the three of them drove to the resort. Situated in the near vicinity were three other police cars waiting on orders from Mike. "How do I have to identify the Langlands? Not face to face, I hope." "No, nothing so confronting. We have booked a unit overlooking the one they are occupying, so it will be a secret identification." Lauren heaved a huge sigh of relief.

They were taken up to the fourteenth floor and shown into a unit. The managers didn't know what was happening, only that a specified unit had been requested. This time no one was going to warn them. The police knew the date the Langlands had left their last apartment, so had enquired who had booked in to this resort on that same day. Only one family had booked in, Mr and Mrs Sullivan and their sick daughter. Now it was up to Lauren. She couldn't wait to see Sally again. Was she okay? was the burning question. She went to the window and the first person she saw was Mrs Langlands. Yes, this was definitely them. Then she spotted the Asian man. "Mike, the Asian guy is with them," reported Lauren. "Right, we will call for back-up straight away," and he got on his phone. Within minutes they all converged on reception asking the manager to disable the lifts. They took the stairwell up to the fourteenth floor. There were a lot of stairs to climb but these men were trained for this type of work. Six men had the unit door covered. Mike knocked on the door and a voice called out asking who was there. "It is the police!" and with that he unlocked the door and barged in. The Asian guy tried to do a runner, but was caught by six burly men in the hallway. Within seconds he found himself in handcuffs. The Langlands just stood in shock, there was no escape for them. Mike searched the bedrooms and found a young girl lying on a bed, heavily drugged. He went to her and recognised her. Thank God, it was Sally. The police handcuffed the Langlands and led them out into the hallway and down the stairwell so they would not be seen. They didn't want to upset other guests. Once they were out of sight Mike called for Lauren to go to Sally, lying drugged on a bed. Lauren was shocked: there she lay but her body was taken over by a seizure and she started to shake violently, so Lauren sat on the bed and held her hand. She wanted to take her in her arms but she would have to wait until the shaking stopped. She was heartbroken, it was horrible watching what drugs did to these young girls. She waited until Sally came back into the real world. Her eyes were starting to focus and when she saw Lauren she smiled. Lauren lifted her up and held her in her arms and they cried together. "I'm taking you away from here, Sally, away from these horrible people. I will look after you and get you better," she promised. "I know you, you are the nice lady from the beach." "Yes, I talked to you on the beach," said Lauren. "You felt warm and nice, I thought about you, but you never came, so I thought it was a dream," sobbed Sally. "Oh Sally, I have missed you, I have been trying to find you, thank God you are safe," cried Lauren as she held her in her arms. This cemented her decision to buy the home. It was the right one, she knew in this moment, that the new path she was taking was to care for these lost souls. Saving lives came before making money. Money was something you spent and yielded no feelings, whereas lives were precious and held warmth.

The police came back, as they had to take Sally to hospital for an assessment to see what damage had been done. She would be there for a couple of days so the doctors could monitor her. They would start her on a drug withdrawal programme. Her first few days were going to be horrendous, she would suffer. She cried as they took her away from Lauren. She didn't want to lose her again, she was the only ray of light at this time in her life. "I will come every day and visit you," Lauren promised, as tears ran down her cheeks. Sally was sobbing as they took her away. Lauren thanked God that this girl had been spared! It was too late to save the first one.

Today Lauren would talk to Anna and tell her what was going to happen to the management rights for this apartment block. She would start at the beginning, about her feelings towards these young girls being used and abused and how it affected her seeing them suffer. She wanted to help them recover and lead near to normal lives again. She felt this was her calling. "I have offered the management rights to Scott and he has accepted. Your job is safe, and I have warned him not to come on to you, as has happened to his receptionists in the past, including me. He knows this business inside out and is a good manager." "Lauren, I'm going to miss you, I know you are following your heart. These girls need someone special like you," Anna assured her. "Sally has no one to care for her when she leaves hospital, I feel a special bond with her, so I must be there for her. Scott will start next week. As soon as my house is finalised, I will move out and he will take over my apartment. You have been a good friend, Anna, so thank you," said a sincere Lauren.

Now it was time to visit Sally. Lauren drove to the hospital and parked in the carpark. She made her way to the front desk, where she asked to see her. She was taken down a long corridor to a gated block. The nurse took the key from her pocket and unlocked the door, then locked it again as they entered. Lauren was horrified. Why all this? she wondered. The ward housed several young girls all in one huge room. They were in various stages of drug rehabilitation. Then she spotted Sally, only to find she was under restraint while lying in the bed. Lauren ran to her with tears streaming down her face. "Sally, it's me, Lauren, are you all right?" "Don't leave me, please stay with me," she sobbed. Lauren took her hand and sat in the chair by her bed. She felt safe having Lauren there, so drifted off to sleep. The nurse explained why Sally was being restrained — she was having seizures, this being part of the withdrawal symptoms, and they didn't want her hurting herself while thrashing around. To Lauren this looked cruel, she wanted to take Sally away from here, to hold her while she was suffering. She needed one-on-one care, but in hospital she was a patient like everyone else. Every now and then she opened her eyes and smiled, as if to let Lauren know that she was aware she was there. But came time for her to leave, she would wait until Sally fell into a deep sleep, then sneak out. Her heart was broken to be leaving this young girl here alone. She would come back tomorrow and sit with her.

The next day when she went to the hospital, Lauren asked if she could speak with the doctor attending Sally. She wanted to know what drugs had been given to her. At this stage, no one knew! The police were still trying to get this information out of the Langlands, but they were not forthcoming with any evidence that might incriminate themselves. The only true answer had to come from Lance, the crooked detective who had defected to the seedy underworld. He was locked in a small cell and until he told what type of drugs they were handling, that was where he would remain. It was up to him!

Lauren walked with the nurse to the rehabilitation ward where the doors were unlocked then locked again as she entered. Today Sally was sitting on her bed. She looked pale and sad, but this soon changed when she saw Lauren. "Did you come yesterday?" she asked. "Yes, Sally, I sat with you for two hours and held your hand, but you kept falling asleep on me. How are you feeling today?" She told Lauren she was a little better, but she couldn't keep her food down. All food had no taste, so she didn't want to eat it. This, of course, was the effect of the drugs, they messed with the palate. She probably hadn't eaten properly for a long period of time, so couldn't remember what food actually tasted like! "Sally, I need to know the real name of those horrible people. Who were they known as, at the church? You did tell me, but I forgot. Do you remember their names?" "Yes, they are the Stuarts, Isla and Robert. That is what they are called there. They go to church every Sunday, everyone thinks they are good people, but they are bad. I know that now, I only wanted to get better," she sobbed. "I know that, pet, but that is all behind you now. We will get you well." Sally put her arms around Lauren and held on tight, she wanted to be with her, she was so kind. Lauren wondered if she felt a sense of security within her arms. Was the warmth she felt for this young soul filtering through to her? Lauren hoped this was so.

# 7

# A shock for the church

This morning was Sunday and Scott was filling in reception for the day. Lauren was at the Salvation Army church service. She was a bit hesitant as she didn't know what to expect, but she would cope as best she could. It was all a bit heavy for her, but then, she was not a churchgoer! After the service everyone mingled, as they all seemed to know each other. Lauren asked the captain that took the service if she could speak with him in private. They went to a little room at the back of the church, where she was asked to sit down. "Thank you. I was wondering if I could talk to you about Isla and Robert Stuart?" "I'm sorry, we don't discuss our members with new parishioners," he told Lauren. "All I want to know is, are they trusted members of your church?" she asked. "Yes, they are very highly thought of, they are big donors to our charities. We have even placed a couple of troubled girls in their care, at their request," he said in high praise of them. "Why do you ask?" Where was she going to start? Obviously, the money they donated played a big part in making them look good. How was she going to tell him it was drug money, and the girls were not looked after, they were abused?

"I want you to listen to what I am going to tell you. It will come as a shock to yourself and your church, but I am speaking the truth. The police will back me up, if you have any doubts. The Stuarts will never be coming back to your church, they will be serving a prison sentence for many years. They are drug dealers, and the young girls you entrusted to them were used as drug mules. The first girl's body was found washed up on the rocks. The most profound thing about this, no one claimed her body. She was someone's daughter, lost forever and alone. The post-mortem showed drugs in her system, and her body had been badly scarred, but it was noted as a drug overdose. The next girl, Sally, is in a secure hospital unit beginning drug rehabilitation. I know your organisation is creditable and helps many people, but the Stuarts used and abused your good name. They used it as a cover-up for their drug dealings. I am sorry to bring you this terrible news, but you had to know."

The poor man just sat with his mouth wide open, he was in shock and speechless. These were some of his parishioners, well liked and well known. They attended church every Sunday and donated generously. But drug money, surely this wasn't what they gave the church! Then his thoughts went to the girls. Kirsty was the daughter of one of his church members. She had veered off the path of righteousness and had been given to the church to find a safe place for her to recuperate. Now she was no longer with them. She was an only child of a wealthy farming couple. He couldn't remember the other girl, but when it all registered with him, he slumped forward in his chair, the burden was too much for him to bear. Lauren jumped up and called for help. Several officers came in and went to his help. "I will leave my card here, and if the captain wants to talk to me, this is where he can contact me," she said, as she left. This was something she wished she didn't have to do, but they had a right to know, as their church's good name was being used in vain. She left there with a heavy heart.

Sally was having a bad day today and had to be restrained in her bed. Coming off drugs was a terrible shock to the body, her mood swings were horrendous and there was nothing they could do about it, it was part of the detox process. The body was not being fed the poison that it had been getting, so it had to make a big adjustment. All Lauren could do was sit with her and hold her hand, so she knew she wasn't on her own, that someone cared for her. She watched as Sally's eyes opened, then rolled, it was heart-wrenching to watch. But if she was going to care for addicts, then she had to know what the healing process yielded and what the girls went through to come out clean at the end. But sadly, not all did! This Lauren would probably learn over time, as not everyone could be saved. She hated the drug underworld, especially when vulnerable boys and girls were exposed to the worst possible life one could ever imagine. They ceased being people, they became possessed by demons. She couldn't wait until the Stuarts were punished. They did the crime, they would do the time!

Lauren had received a call from Mike. He wanted to take her out for a surprise dinner tonight. He would pick her up at five o'clock at her apartment. She was thankful she could call on Scott for reception duties, as this was the first time she had taken a full day off for what seemed like forever. It was only one more week before he took over the

management and Lauren could move into her newly pur-
chased home. It needed to be painted inside so one day
soon, she would pick out happy colours and get stuck in.
She was excited to be going out with Mike tonight. She
showered and spent a bit of well-earned time on herself;
she wanted to look nice for him. Time had not been her
friend lately, it seemed to belong to everyone else and very
little was left for her. She had no idea where she was going,
but of course she hadn't asked.

When he arrived, Mike was all dressed up in a suit and
Lauren was surprised. He scrubbed up well, and she let
him know this. In fact, he was a real hunk of a man. She
was happy it was her on his arm tonight, but where were
they going? Mike escorted her to his car and they drove up
to Broadbeach and pulled into the carpark at the Grand
Hotel. Gosh, this is posh, Lauren thought. She leaned over
and kissed him on the cheek. "Come, my little minx, this
night belongs to you!" and he led her into a huge reception
area, then they were shown through to a large dining
room. As Lauren looked around, she could see a few familiar faces. What was going on? As they walked to their seats
at the head of a long table, everyone started clapping. Lauren felt embarrassed. Then silence reigned. "Tonight, we
would like to welcome you, Lauren, to dine with us as
our special guest of honour, for your important input into
taking down a significant drug syndicate. Many men have
worked on this project, which started nearly a year ago,
but this cartel was always one step ahead of us. It is thanks
to you, Lauren, and your alertness that led us to these
arrests, so we all want to say a big thank you." The clapping started again, much to Lauren's embarrassment, so
she tried to hide behind Mike to escape the limelight. She
was in shock, never in her wildest dreams did she think

this was going to happen. So much for a quiet night out! She leaned over to Mike and whispered, "Why didn't you tell me this was going to happen?" "Then it wouldn't have been a surprise." They had a wonderful night and everyone came up to her and congratulated her. The night certainly belonged to her, just as Mike had promised.

Five days had passed since Lauren had visited the Salvation Army church service and spoke with the captain. Today she received a phone call asking her to come to their headquarters the next morning at eleven o'clock. She wondered what they wanted. Hadn't she brought them enough bad news? Perhaps they didn't believe what she had told them, and who could blame them? It was something no one would want to hear, especially not a place of worship. She would have to put aside her packing, as she was getting ready for her shift in less than a week. It was going to be exciting to move into her own home. Lauren couldn't wait to start painting and preparing her house for her first guest, who was, of course, Sally. She looked at her watch. It was time for her visit to the hospital, as Sally would be waiting for her. What would she find today?

Just when everything seemed to be on track, there were always down days, and it seemed as if they had to go back to the start. Would today be different? Lauren was learning something new each day. She would record everything in her little book — this she would use as her bible and it would be used as her directory for future references. She pulled up at the carpark and walked to the hospital foyer and was surprised to see Sally sitting in a seat waiting for her. She wasn't behind the locked door. "Hi, Lauren, you're late" was what greeted her. This made her smile, Sally just said what came into her head at that very moment. "Only you would have a clock on me!" she answered. "Can we walk around the grounds, Lauren? I'm feeling better, that's why I'm not locked up. I'm free today, well, for a little while." With this she reached for Lauren's hand. 'I'm free': these two words echoed in Lauren's mind, fancy thinking to be out from behind locked hospital doors was freedom, it almost sounded like she was doing a prison sentence. "Soon, my pet, we will be walking along the beach together, that is freedom," Lauren told her. "Will we always be friends?" she asked. "I hope so, Sally. We will be living together and I will be your guardian angel. I will care for you as if you were my own daughter. I made a promise to you and I will never break that promise." "You are still that nice lady from the beach who I dreamt about all that time. Now you are here with me. I like you, Lauren," she said, as tears filled her eyes. They walked around the grounds holding hands, nothing much else was said, it had all been said in those few words. Just for Sally to know someone was there for her was all that mattered, she was happy. When it was time to say good-bye, Sally cried, "Come back tomorrow, Lauren, I'll be waiting for my angel!" Lauren took her in her arms and held her tight. "Sleep well, my pet, I can't wait till tomorrow, I won't be late!" She waved to Sally as she climbed into her car.

Lauren arrived at the Salvation Army headquarters. As she climbed out of her car, she was asked to come to an office where the captain was waiting for her. He shook her hand and asked her to sit down. "Thank you for our last meeting, I am sorry I didn't say goodbye, but I was in shock. It took me several days to digest that information you gave to me. They were trusted members of our church. But why I have requested for you to come today is to meet Mr and Mrs Clarke. They are the parents of the young girl that drowned. They have lost their only child and are distraught. They want to speak to you, as you were the last person to see their daughter alive." "But the condition I saw her in was so sad, how can I tell them? It will break their hearts even further. She was drugged, she was not human any more. I'm sorry but I can't do this," said Lauren. "But you must, Lauren, I have told them what had happened to her, but they want to hear it from you. They want closure and you are the only person that can do that. I know how hard it will be, but it is God's wish that you help them through their darkest moments. I feel a lot of the blame, as I placed her with the Stuarts. Together we must help these people." What could she do when it was put to her like this?

Lauren was in shock. What was she going to tell these parents, how would they take it, would they be able to cope with the truth? But she couldn't lie; panic took over. The captain rung a little bell and the door opened, in walked a couple, so Lauren stood up and held out her hand. "Lauren, meet Mr and Mrs Clarke." They shook hands and then they sat down. "This is going to be sad for both parties, particularly you, Lauren, so I will leave you to talk in private," said the captain, as he stood up and walked to the door. They sat and looked at each other, then the tears started. "I am so sorry for what has happened, but I was too late to save your daughter. By the time I fully realised what was going on, she disappeared that very night," Lauren told them among her tears. "Please tell us what you know about Kirsty. We have brought a photo of her for you to see." They handed Lauren the photo. What a beautiful young girl, just looking at the image set her off. Tears flowed as she remembered the girl crouched in the lift drugged out of her brain.

All she could do was relay to Kirsty's parents what had happened to her. She told them about the drug drop-offs and pick-ups she was expected to do at nights on her own while she was drugged. When Lauren discovered this, it was only a couple of nights later that her backpack had been found washed up on the beach. The next morning her body was found washed up on the rocks in the next bay. The postmortem proved there was no foul play, just that she had drugs in her system. "What do you think happen to her?" asked Mr Clarke. "I think she just wanted to end the life she was living so walked into the water to find a more peaceful existence. The life she is living now has freed her of all her hurt. The hurt is still with you, but she is at peace and if you can accept this it will help you mend. The Stuarts recruited another young girl the next day, but of course they didn't know what happened to Kirsty, they probably thought she had absconded with the drugs." "What of the next girl?" asked Mrs Clarke. "She was the lucky one, I rescued her when the police took the Stuarts away. She is in a hospital in a secure unit undergoing drug rehabilitation, then she is coming to live with me. I have opened my home as a refuge for these young girls who have been preyed upon and lured into the seedy underworld of drugs. They are lost souls. Sally will be my first guest. I can't wait to get her home and care for her, she is just like a child. Her brain has been poisoned, but I will nurse and love her. I am so sorry I couldn't save your daughter, the world she left behind was cruel. Please take home your happy memories of her and know she is in a better place," sobbed Lauren. They could see that Lauren was profoundly upset. "How can we thank you? We will set up a charity to help you run your home for our lost daughters. We need people like you. You will need finances so we will look after this for you. Every other daughter out there is just as important as ours, so thank you, Lauren, you have brought closure to us. We will keep in touch."

When the meeting had finished, the captain came back into the room. "I am still reeling over how the Stuarts operated an illegal business, right under our nose, and to use our church as a cover-up is even more upsetting. They have taken the Lord's name in vain. But those young girls, we did them an injustice. They will not be forgotten, we will pray for them every Sunday. As you now know Kirsty came from a farming background, her parents are very wealthy, and now they have lost their only child, they have indicated they will help your cause. The mother's pain is with her every day and because of this, she is pleased to know that you will help other young girls who are troubled, so they will fundraise for you. You are a noble young lady, Lauren, we wish you well. Goodbye for now, we will keep in touch." Lauren thanked him and left the building.

What a draining start to her day! Lauren was on her way to visit Sally. Hopefully she will cheer me up, she thought. She had to squeeze this visit in before going on reception at five o'clock. Today Sally was not at the door waiting for her. What was wrong? The nurse told her Sally was having a bad day. She hadn't stopped crying since she woke this morning, but she wouldn't say why! She took Lauren to the locked door and let her in, then locked it again. As Lauren made her way to Sally's bed, there she was, lying face down sobbing. "What is wrong, my little angel?" she asked. She sat up and cuddled into Lauren. "Why am I in here? I haven't done anything wrong. I don't like it here any more. Why am I locked in? Please take me home with you, Lauren?" she pleaded. "I would love to, Sally, but I have to go to work. In three days' time I will be moving into our home, then you can come and live with me. Only three more days, let's count them together … one, two, three …" "But that's a long time," she said. By now the sobbing had stopped. "Tell me your favourite colour and I will get the paint and we will paint your room together when you come home," Lauren told her. "I like yellow, it's warm like the sun. That would mean the sun would shine all the time, wouldn't that be cool, Lauren?" she asked. Now she was starting to perk up. There was no stimulation here for her any more, she needed to be out in the real world, not in a hospital room behind locked doors. All this would come to an end in three days, but to Sally that was a lifetime!

# 8

# A new friendship

Today was the day Lauren was given the keys to her home. She had finished at the apartments last night, now it was up to Scott and Anna. Because she didn't have a lot of furniture, Scott had kindly offered her what he didn't need, as he was taking over Lauren's fully furnished apartment. She had one full day before Sally arrived, so she had to buy beds, dressers and linen. Now that she knew Sally's favourite colour was yellow, it made it a lot easier for her to choose linen for her room. They would paint it together, this would be their first project. Lauren felt this was the first day of a new life for her, one where she could share her love with those girls who needed it. She felt happy within herself and to have Sally with her from tomorrow was going to be her first challenge along with her biggest blessing. She knew what it was like to feel trapped, unable to leave. It took away the freedom of life, and what life stood for, in fact it robbed one of life. But to live behind a locked door, be it a hospital or a prison, there was no difference. All thought of a future slowly diminished. It was a feeling of entrapment!

Everything was looking spick and span, Lauren felt proud. The furniture had been delivered and Mike helped her put things where she wanted them. This was the first time, while setting up a home, that she was able to make her own decisions about where things should be placed, and it was a wonderful feeling. She was her own self, not ruled by anyone! That was why she told Scott he was not to mess with Anna, she was out of bounds, no way did she want her caught up in his tangled web. Outwardly he was a nice person, but inwardly he was very possessive, almost to the point of having a low self-esteem, therefore he got his power by becoming the dominant one, the owner of his victim. But that was then ... this was now!

Sally's bedroom was all set up and it looked lovely, apart from the walls, but these would be painted in the next couple of days, as the paint was ready and waiting. Lauren had bought a nice duvet and frilly pillowcases to match, and had placed cushions on the bed and on the rocking chair she had bought as a special present for Sally. Now it was time to set up her own bed. Mike helped her put it together and when it was ready, they both had to lie on it to see if it was comfortable. It felt that good, they didn't want to get off it. Then it had to be tested for bounce, yes, this was the perfect love nest! Hopefully it would be used often for that very purpose.

Lauren never got to visit Sally today as she had so much to do, but she had told her yesterday that she might not make it. Hopefully she remembered and didn't wait for her. Her memory was slowly coming back. It had all but gone, the drugs had stolen this from her, placing her in a world of non-existence, where the brain was virtually in shutdown mode. She would be on medication for another couple of months, then hopefully she would be able to function on her own. Lauren didn't realise that rehabilitation was such a lengthy process. Perhaps it was wise to take girls who were over the worst week or so, after they were released from hospital? Time would tell, it would be a matter of trial and error!

The big day had arrived! Lauren was so excited she was bringing Sally home, where she would have one-on-one love and care. She would leave earlier than usual, because she had to have a meeting with the hospital personnel re Sally's medication and fill out her release papers. Once this was all signed off Lauren was taken along the corridor to the locked doors. Standing there banging on the doors was Sally, demanding to be let out. When she saw Lauren, she burst into tears. "I've been waiting here all night for you to come, Lauren, you are late!" "No, it was always today," she said. But then time and dates ran together for these girls, reality still wasn't quite there with them. "I'm here now. Are you ready to come home?" she asked. "Take me away from these locked doors, I haven't done anything wrong," she sobbed. She had a thing about locked doors. Did she think she was bad and this was why she was put behind them? Lauren couldn't wait to get Sally out of the hospital. Everyone had done what was required of them and looked after her, but she was ready for the real world, where she could feel free — no more locked doors!

As they pulled up at Lauren's house, Sally was really excited. She could hear the waves pounding on the beach and see the sand. "Is this our home, Lauren? Gosh, it's nice," she said as she got out of the car. She took Lauren's hand and they walked inside. Sally walked through the house and spotted the yellow bed linen in one of the rooms. "Is this mine?" "Yes, this is your bedroom, but remember we are going to paint it yellow," replied Lauren. "Then the sun will shine every day in my room and it will make me feel happy." Lauren loved the way she expressed how she felt, as her feelings were being released. This was a good start! "Can we go for a walk on the sand? Take your shoes off, Lauren, and we will walk in our bare feet." Then she ran down the path, opened the gate, and headed down to the water. Lauren followed shoeless and when she caught up with her, Sally took her hand and they ran along the beach together. "Do you feel free, Sally?" Lauren asked. "Yes, I hate locked doors. To leave them behind I felt free, but this is really free," she laughed.

They continued along the beach, when suddenly she let go of Lauren's hand and knelt down in the sand and started digging with her bare hands. "What are you digging for, Sally?" I don't know, I used to do this. Was I looking for something?" she asked with a puzzled look on her face. Lauren's heart stopped for a minute. Were these memories always going to haunt her? Should she hide them from her, or explain her actions? She didn't want there to be any hidden secrets between them, so best tell the truth. "Remember when I found you, Sally, I told you that you were working for people who sold drugs. This is what you used to do, bury them for those horrible people." "Why would I do that? That's silly." "You didn't know what you were doing, because they drugged you. You just did as you were told," replied Lauren. "Where are they now?" "They are locked up behind bars, waiting to come before the courts, then they will be sent to prison for a very long time," she explained. "Is that why I was behind a locked door, because of drugs?" Lauren explained to Sally her situation was different, she was coming off drugs, and it was a very painful process. "You are on the road to recovery, that is why I want to be with you, so I can help you. I cried when I first saw you, Sally, you were so sick I just had to rescue you, but it took a long time to get you away. But here we are, both happy." "I remembered you told me you were my guardian angel, that's why you rescued me. You must have liked me, Lauren?" and with this she grabbed her hand. Not another word was spoken as they ran back towards the house.

Sadly, there weren't two girls here today. She was too late to save the other girl and this played on her mind. She would tell Sally about it one day, when the time was right. They both fell into an armchair and it wasn't long before Sally nodded off. Lauren brought a cover over and tucked her in. She sat and watched, she seemed happy enough. So far everything had gone to plan. Lauren did wonder what she liked to eat, as they had not discussed food. The hospital said she ate very little, but this was not good for her. She had to eat to get healthy again. She was pale and skinny, not a good look. She would get her to write down her favourite foods, then she would know what to cook. It was no good cooking things that she didn't like, this would hinder, not help her situation. It would be a learning curve for them both!

Lauren was pottering around in the kitchen, as she was still finding places to put her cooking utensils. She had tried to buy plates and cups with yellow flowers or patterns on them, as this might help Sally with her eating. She knew it wasn't going to be easy. Two hours had passed and Sally was just stirring. It took several minutes for her to get her bearings. "Lauren, I think I have been asleep for a couple of minutes," she called out. "Yes, you dozed off on me, but that's okay. I want you to write a list of your favourite foods so I know what to cook for you," and with this she handed Sally a pen and note paper. She watched and waited but Sally just sat there staring at the paper. What was going through her mind? wondered Lauren, nothing was being written down. "Why is it so hard to write your favourite foods?" she asked. "I can't remember, I haven't eaten much for a long time. You just cook me something and I will see if I can eat it." Poor Lauren was no further ahead. How sad not to know what food you liked, but as she thought back, she probably wasn't fed food, only drugs. She remembered the hospital had said she ate very little and could not afford to lose any more weight, as she was skin and bone. "I will cook you an omelette, I know you will like that, because it is yellow." With this came a giggle.

Sally stood and watched as Lauren prepared the omelette. She was right, it was yellow! She made a side salad to go with it. They both sat down to eat. Sally took one bite and held it in her mouth for a few minutes before swallowing it. She was trying to work out a taste, as her palate had gone to sleep. The acid from the drugs had taken its toll, destroying all that was natural in one's body. She took a long time to eat her food, but she managed to empty her plate. "Did you enjoy that?" asked Lauren, knowing she had struggled. "Thank you, Lauren, you are a good cook." Then she asked Sally if she would like a yoghurt for dessert, but she didn't know what it was. She went and fetched one each from the refrigerator. Sally watched as Lauren pulled the lid off and gave her a teaspoon to eat it with. When she finished, she asked, "Can I have another one?" "Why do you like that?" asked Lauren. "It is slippery in my mouth, then it falls down my throat easy, I like it." So now she knew to give Sally moist food. Perhaps something had happened to her throat — she would ask at the hospital next time she went.

After tea they sat on the settee together and watched TV. Lauren found a comedy and they both had a good laugh. She wanted Sally to go to bed feeling happy. She asked her if she wanted to shower at night or in the morning, to which she chose the morning. "Tomorrow we are going to paint your walls, so we will start first thing." "Do we have breakfast first?" Sally asked. "Of course, what would you like?" "I'm having yoghurt, that's my favourite," was her answer. Having sorted this out, she decided she was ready for bed. Lauren told her to call out when she was in bed and she would come in and say goodnight. Only a few minutes went by and Lauren received the call. That was quick, she thought. When she went in, Sally was in bed in her clothes. "Where are your pyjamas?" she asked. "I don't have any, there is nothing much in my bag." Oh my God. Lauren had never given a thought to her clothing, she had just presumed ... so she had a look in her bag. All she could see was a couple of pairs of knickers, jeans and a jumper. "Is that all you have?" she asked. "I don't know if I have other clothes, where would they be?" This left Lauren dumbfounded and wondering what she wore in hospital, but, of course, they supplied gowns. "Right, tomorrow before we start painting, we are going shopping. Tonight, you can wear a pair of my pyjamas, you are not going to sleep in your clothes," and she went and fetched her a pair. "You're bossy, Lauren," came back the reply. Lauren left the room while she changed into the pyjamas and jumped into bed, again! "I'm ready this time," she called. "Your pyjamas are huge on me," was what greeted Lauren as she came back into her room. This made her laugh, she did have a sense of humour, whether she knew it or not. She came over and sat on her bed. "I hope you will be happy here with me, Sally, I will look after you, then one day when you are better, you will find a life of your own." "No, I'm going to stay with you forever," she said in all earnestness. With this Lauren leaned over and kissed her on the forehead. "This is my first kiss, Lauren, thank you!" Lauren had to turn away as tears streamed down her cheeks. Fancy this being her first kiss at aged … what? She didn't even know how old she was, but that could wait until tomorrow. She locked up and went to her bed.

Lauren was up twice during the night to settle Sally, as she was calling out in her sleep. She lay on her bed and rubbed her forehead soothing her and letting her know she was not alone. But she did expect this — the hospital staff had warned her this might happen. It was caused by the drugs altering their sleep pattern, their life become unbalanced. This depended on the dosage and the type of drugs they were taking, as the body clock slowed down and time was no longer relevant. One day ran into the next, and on it went.

When Lauren woke in the morning she went straight to Sally's room, but it was empty, she was gone! She ran back to her room and pulled on some clothes, then searched the house. No Sally! The front door was unlocked so she ran down the path, opened the gate and shouted as she ran onto the beach. She could see people everywhere, which one was her? Lauren felt sick. She continued along the sand calling her name, then she saw a man and a girl further on. As she came closer, yes, it was Sally, but who was the man? She stopped and watched for a moment, taking particular notice of the male. Then she saw him hand something to Sally. Lauren didn't know if she should approach him. Was he a drug dealer trying to recruit vulnerable young girls? She stood her distance until he left, then she called to Sally. She ran to Lauren and put her arms around her. "What did that man want, did you know him?" she asked. "He gave me something to take, he said it would make me feel better. How did he know I was sick?" she asked in all innocence. "But do you know him?" questioned Lauren. "No, he just asked if he could meet me again." "Please give me what he gave you!" she demanded. "Don't be bossy, Lauren!" "Sally, you must never leave the house in the morning or any other time on your own. You have been a very sick girl and you are still recovering. The stuff in that packet is probably drugs, this is how you young girls get sick. He is a bad man, that is why he wants to meet you again, hoping you will want more, then he will ask you to do things for him. Young girls walking the beach on their own are targeted by these bad men. I will give this to Mike and he will get it tested." "Who is Mike?" she asked. Lauren told her that he was her boyfriend. "Do I know him?" She explained he was the one who helped rescue her from the Stuarts. "You must promise me you will never leave the house on your own again, Sally," Lauren told her. "Yes, bossy Lauren," and she hung her head and grabbed her hand.

Lauren picked up the phone and rang Mike and asked him if he could come over, she had to speak with him about what had just happened. After eating her favourite breakfast, the yoghurt she had eaten for the first time last night and today was her favourite, Sally was on the dishes. Lauren decided they would paint Sally's bedroom walls while they were waiting on Mike to arrive. Shopping would have to wait until later. Lauren spread on old sheet on the floor, after they had moved the bed to one side.

She mixed up the paint and prepared the rollers. After giving Sally instructions, she climbed the ladder and painted along the top so all Sally had to do was roll the roller down the wall. A simple job turned into a nightmare! Sally was all over the place with the roller, she didn't seem to have any idea what straight meant. But all this aside, she thought she was doing great. "Isn't this fun. Lauren? I love painting, we should do the whole house," she suggested. Lauren didn't hear this, she turned a deaf ear. Now it was time to go over her work and repaint the missed pieces. "What are you doing that for? You're too fussy, Lauren." Now they were on to the next wall. This time she gave Sally a demo on how it was to be done properly. By lunch time it was finished. "Gosh, Lauren, we are good painters, but you are still bossy," she said and they both laughed. Once everything was put back in its place, the room look bright and fresh. "See, I told you the sun would shine in my room if we painted it yellow," said a proud young girl.

For lunch, Lauren made Sally a tomato and cheese sandwich. She was hungry after doing the painting, so ate it without any comments. Perhaps if she gave her things to use up her energy, she would feel hungry. She had to start eating larger meals to build up her body mass, as it had started to waste away. Just as they were finishing eating, there was a knock on the door. Sally ran to open it and there stood a strange man. "Who are you? Do you know Lauren?" she asked. "Hello, Sally, I'm Mike, lovely to meet you." "Oh, you are Lauren's boyfriend, you can come in," then she yelled, "Lauren, it's your boyfriend!" Mike was amused listening to this introduction, such innocence! He walked over to Lauren and took her in his arms. "Missed me?" he asked. Lauren asked Sally to clear the table and wash the dishes. "Yes, bossy Lauren," she answered.

She wanted to talk to Mike about the man who had approached Sally on the beach and to find out what was in the packet he had given her. He was horrified that this had happened right here on this stretch of beach, as this area was classed by the police as pretty safe. Nearer Surfers it was known for its dealers, but down here was a surprise. "Would you know the man if you saw him again?" he asked. Lauren said she thought she would. Mike explained they would have to get him off the beach as he was a danger to vulnerable teenagers. He was obviously looking for recruitments for his drug dealing. "We have to catch him in the act. Do you think we could let Sally walk ahead of us and see if he approaches her again?" he asked. Lauren was not happy about this. She didn't want Sally involved ever again with anything to do with drugs. She hated that word!

Mike said he would arrange for undercover police to be stationed along the beach and one signal from him, they would close in and arrest him. These scumbags had to be removed if other girls were to be safe. Lauren said she would have to think about it, but it didn't take long for her to agree. Her thoughts had drifted back to the girl whose body was washed up on the rocks and the heartache the parents were going through, hence the quick decision. "You let me know when you can get the back-up and we will work in with you." Mike couldn't wait to take the packet back to the station and have it analysed.

That night Mike came back to Lauren's home. He had found out what was in the packet. It was a lethal home-made concoction, one that would have serious side effects on the user. They had held a discussion at the station and tomorrow was the day, as these toxic pills had to be taken off the market as soon as possible, otherwise there would be some very sick people. He asked Lauren if he could stay the night, of course she said yes. Now they would sit together and tell Sally of tomorrow's plans. Mike explained what was in the package the man had given her, that it was a harmful drug. "Then why did he give it me?" she sobbed. "Because, Sally, you were alone on the beach. This is what these bad people do, they find young girls like you, then give them drugs and they become hooked on them, they can't do without them, so they take more. Then they control you and make you deliver packages to strange places," Mike explained. "Like me, I buried things in the sand. Lauren told me what I did, isn't that silly, but I don't remember," Sally said in all innocence. "That is why we must catch them and lock them up. Tomorrow morning, Lauren and I will walk along the beach with you, but we will be just behind you. We want to see if that man comes up to you again. If he gives you another packet, I want you to take it. Don't be frightened, we will be right behind you. Do you think you could do this, Sally?" "Is it all right for me to do this, Lauren?" she asked. "Yes, Sally, we will be helping to save girls like yourself, but only if you think you can do it, there is no pressure. If you are not happy, you don't have to do it." Sally thought for a minute, then agreed, but she said she would be frightened.

They all sat and watched TV until Sally announced she was going to bed. "Lauren, we forgot to go shopping today. Damn, I'll have to wear your huge pyjamas again tonight. When are you going home?" she asked Mike. "I'm staying with Lauren tonight." "Which room are you going to sleep in?" she asked. Lauren answered, "He is staying in my room with me." "But he's a man, he can't stay in your room!" Lauren was shocked. How much did this innocent mind know? Obviously not a lot. "How old are you, Sally?"

she asked. "I think I'm seventeen or eighteen, I don't know, you tell me?" "I don't know either, we will find out tomorrow, now off to bed and no more questions." A little mutter was heard as she left the room: "Okay, bossy Lauren." Mike and Lauren couldn't hold their laughter any longer, she was so young and innocent for her age, no more than a child really. Five minutes passed and the call was heard. "I'm ready." Lauren went in and tucked her in and kissed her on the forehead. "That is kiss number two, thank you, Lauren." "Goodnight, my angel. Remember, never leave this house again without me."

The walk was to take place before breakfast, as it was about this time it had happened. Lauren hugged Sally and told her not to worry, they were just behind her. The three of them walked along separately but close enough to call to each other. Then it all unfolded before their eyes. A man approached Sally and asked her if she wanted another packet, then handed it to her. This was when Mike did his signal and the plain-clothed police descended upon the man. Lauren ran to Sally and took her in her arms while this was all happening. Sally still had the packet in her hand. Mike came and took it from her. "You were very brave, Sally, thank you," he praised her. "Is Mike a policeman?" she asked. Lauren told her, yes, he was in the police force. Now it was time for them to walk back and have some breakfast. Mike did not come, he went back to the station with the arrested man. He wanted to see if these drugs were the same as the last lot.

The girls hit the shops. It was time for Lauren to buy Sally some clothes. They went to a department store to have a look at dresses, tops and jeans. Sally flittered from one rack to the next, but nothing escaped her eye, before asking how many things she was allowed. "You pick out what you like and try them on, then we will decide." She was like a little girl in a candy shop. No one would ever have guessed her age, she was very immature, but how many years was she without parental guidance? How old was she when she left her family home and entered the seedy underworld of drugs? As Lauren looked at her, she wondered if anyone had taken advantage of her body. Would she have known if she was drugged? This terrible thought had just come to her mind. "Wake up, Lauren, what do you think?" she asked. Lauren was quickly brought back to reality. Sally had selected what she liked and that was good enough for Lauren. She wasn't going to restrict her thinking, nothing was outrageous, or even a little bit revealing, it was just plain normal.

Sally walked out of the shop with a part wardrobe of new clothes. "Thank you, bossy Lauren," she said as she hugged her. Next was to a lingerie shop, but this proved a far more difficult task. Sally picked out a couple of pretty bras, but the lady wanted her to try them on before she bought them, but she flatly refused. "Can I take them home and try them on there?" she asked. "But Sally, you must try them on in the shop, this is shop policy," intervened Lauren. Sally flatly refused and walked out of the shop. Lauren called for her to come back in. "Come into the changing room and I will have a look at the tag on your bra, it will tell us the size." They went into the changing room where Lauren lifted up Sally's top and was shocked to see her back was covered in scars — some were still quite raw. They looked horrible. How did they get there? She didn't mention them to Sally, she just found the tag and took the size. No wonder she didn't want the assistant to be of any help to her, she would have felt ashamed. Now they knew what they were after, Sally picked some pretty ones. "These are nice, Lauren; do you wear pretty ones too?" she asked. Lauren laughed at this remark. Next on the list were pyjamas, of which she bought three pairs and they were a smaller size. "Now I won't have to wear your huge ones, Lauren," she told her. She found nice knickers to match her bras so was a happy girl.

Next came the shoe department. The only shoes she had were a well-worn pair of sneakers that had seen better days. This was where the hardest decisions had to be made. Sally loved shoes, she was in her element. By the time she had to make up her mind, there were shoes every-where. What a nightmare she had created for the shop assistant, but she was very patient with her. She could see she wasn't your normal type of girl, there was something strange about her. She was very excitable, perhaps she was a little hyperactive? When Sally eventually made up her mind, they left with five pairs of shoes. If she had her own way, she would have walked out with twelve pairs. "We will be back," were Sally's passing words to the assis-tant. Lauren whispered under her breath, "Not for a long while." She smiled and thanked the shop lady. She could see the lady was puzzled by Sally's actions, but that was none of her business. If only she knew what this young girl had gone through, but she didn't!

Sally staggered into the house with some of her parcels. She had tried to carry them all together, but this didn't work, so she had to make several trips. "Gosh, Lauren, we must have spent a lot of money," she said as she looked at all the parcels. "That's for me to worry about. You just enjoy!" Sally went to her room and closed the door. She was probably going to try them all on again? Lauren's mind went back to the scars on Sally's back. What would have caused them? They looked quite recent, as they were still red and swollen. Where did this happen? While Sally was in her room, Lauren rang the hospital and asked to speak to the nurse that discharged Sally. "Did you notice any sores or scars on Sally's body?" she asked. The nurse told Lauren she wouldn't let anyone near her body, she always went to the bathroom when she wanted to change, so no one would have picked up on this. Then she remembered to ask if they knew Sally's age, but this had also drawn a blank. Lauren thanked her. She would talk to Mike about Sally's scars. Someone had obviously mistreated her, in fact inflicted pain on her, but who?

Later in the day Mike arrived with the analysis on the second lot of drugs that had been given to Sally. They were different to the first ones, so someone was using different ingredients, or they were got from another dealer, but both were lethal! This had to be stopped. The man would appear in the court tomorrow, as it was vital that action was taken straight away to get these dangerous drugs out of circulation. Lauren told Mike about the scars on Sally's back. He was horrified to think she had suffered more pain, other than drugs. He picked up his phone and rang the mortuary to see if the postmortem on the body of the drowned girl revealed anything other than drugs. There had been a mention of scars on her back and buttocks. This verified to Mike that these girls had been tortured at the hands of a cruel dealer. What would he have done to them? Mike asked Lauren to talk to Sally, as it certainly wasn't self-inflicted. The girls couldn't have reached those parts of their bodies themselves. Someone had hurt them, but how and why?

Tonight, as Lauren and Sally were curled up on the settee together watching television, Lauren decided to mention the scars on her back. Were they on her buttocks too?

she wondered?. "Sally, what has happened to your back? You have scars. How did they get there?" "Where did you see them?" she said defensively. "I saw them when I looked for the tag on your bra, in the shop today." "You weren't meant to see them, no one is allowed to see them," she snapped. "What do you mean? I care for you, Sally. Has someone hurt you? Please tell me how they got there?" "I can't, I'm not allowed," she sobbed. "I'm going to bed now, I'm tired," and away she went. Lauren waited until Sally had time to get into bed, then went in to say goodnight to her. She was lying under the blankets sobbing. "Please, Sally, show them to me, I need to see them," and with this Sally lifted up her pyjama top so Lauren could see them. "Do you have any more?" and with this she pulled down her pyjama pants to reveal more on her buttocks. "Someone has hurt you, please tell me what they have done to you?" pleaded Lauren. "No, I will never tell, leave me alone," she sobbed. Lauren bent down and kissed her forehead. "Thank you, bossy Lauren," she said amid her tears. As Lauren left the room, she could hear Sally sobbing. Was she reliving that horror that had been inflicted on her, but what had they done to her?

Lauren turned off the television and lay on the settee trying to recall anything from her days at the apartments that might help her understand what might have happened. Then she remembered several times seeing the girls at various times huddled in a corner. What was done to them? Was this the punishment, were these wounds inflicted on them before they went to the corner, or was this pain about to be dealt to them and they were petrified as to what was going to happen? Lauren felt sick. Why wouldn't Sally talk to her? She picked up her phone to talk to Mike and tell him what she had just seen; it wasn't what she wanted to see. Sally had scars on her buttocks as well as her back. "I wonder what they did to the girls. You met the Langlands, did they look as if they were those types of people?" Mike asked. "No, Mrs Langlands was very sweet, but then they were drug dealers, perhaps that was a cover-up? Oh, I have just thought of something! There were times when an Asian guy was alone with the girls, could he be the culprit? Surely he didn't abuse them, is that why Sally is so frightened? Perhaps he threatened her if she told anyone. I don't think Sally will ever tell." Mike told her to leave it with him, he would think of something.

"Come and stay with me tomorrow night, I've missed you," whispered Lauren. "What will little miss have to say about that? She will probably tell me to go home," said Mike, and they both laughed. Lauren went to bed, her head spinning. It wouldn't let go of the thought of cruelty that the girls had endured. Lauren wasn't long in bed when she heard Sally calling out in her sleep, so she ran to see if she was all right. She was fighting with someone, telling them to leave her alone, not to touch her. Was she reliving the horror she had been through, had Lauren stirred up her feelings by asking questions? She sat on her bed and rubbed her forehead until she seemed settled. Then she made her way back to her bed. But her peace didn't last long. She was woken by someone climbing into her bed. It was Sally and she was shaking violently. "Hold me, Lauren, he is hurting me," she was crying out. "Who is hurting you?" she asked, hoping she would tell her, but nothing more was said. She held her in her arms and they both dropped off to sleep.

As Sally stirred, she was surprised to find Lauren lying beside her. "Wake up, Lauren, why am I here, how did I get in your bed?" she asked. "You were dreaming so you came to my bed." "What was I dreaming about?" she asked. Was this the time to do a little quizzing? "A man was hurting you, you told him to leave you alone. Who is this man, Sally?" "I don't remember," and it was left at that. It was a closed book. One clue came from this: it was definitely a man, but who? Sally made her way back to her own bed and wrapped herself in her bedcover and went to sleep.

Today was Sunday and Lauren thought she might take Sally to church at the Salvation Army hall. Perhaps something there might trigger her memory, as this was where it all started, when she went there for help. "Get dressed into something nice today," she called to Sally. "Where are we going?" "You will just have to wait and see, it's a surprise," Lauren called back. When she came out, she was wearing one of her new dresses and a pair of her new shoes. "You look nice today," remarked Lauren. "I know that," came back an answer. They had breakfast and cleaned up, then made their way to the car. As much as she pleaded with Lauren to tell her where they were going, she would not give in. When they pulled up outside the church hall, she heard Sally say, "Surely not church, Lauren, I've been here before and it's boring." "I wanted to go to church today, I haven't been for a long time, it will do us both good," she said. "Church doesn't do good, it didn't do me good," said Sally. "What do you mean?" asked Lauren. "This is where I met the Stuarts, they didn't do me good, they made me sick." "I'm sorry, Sally, I didn't realise, do you want to leave? We will go home?" "May as well suffer now that we are here," was her reply. They made their way into the hall and sat in a seat near the back of the church, so as not to be noticed. Lauren had to admit it was a bit boring and was relieved when it was over.

As they were leaving, one of the church captains came

up to Lauren and thanked her for attending. "Hello, Lauren," a voice called from behind her and she looked around to find the parents of the girl who had drowned. "We were coming to see you today, as we have a cheque for you. We have been fundraising money for you to care for our girls. How is everything going?" they asked. "I would like you to meet Sally, she is in my care. She is the young girl who was recruited after your daughter, she was the lucky one, thank God," said Lauren. "Hello, Sally, you are a very lucky young lady to have met Lauren. We wish our daughter had met her," they said. "Why, what happened?" she asked. "Perhaps Lauren will tell you one day," said the lady through her tears. "Why are you crying, did I say something wrong?" she asked in all her innocence. The lady came up to Sally and took her in her arms and whispered to her, "Thank God you were spared, my little angel." She could see Sally was still recovering from her trauma. "Can we come and visit another day, we would like to see you again, Sally?" Lauren told them to come any time, they would be most welcome. They handed Lauren a cheque for $5,000. She thanked them and was humbled by their efforts of kindness.

When they arrived home, Mike was already there. "How did you get into our house?" was Sally's greeting to him. "Lauren gave me a key, is that okay with you?" he asked. "Suppose so, if Lauren said." "You look special today, where have you been?" "To boring old church, but we did meet some nice people, didn't we, Lauren? They gave you some money. Why did she call me an angel?" she asked. "Because she likes you," was Lauren's reply. "Don't forget she said you have to tell me something one day, because I might forget?" This brought laughter from both Mike and Lauren. "How would you like to go to McDonald's for tea?" Mike asked Sally. "Yes, please," was her answer. He told her to change, as they would go for a walk along the beach first then head to McDonald's. She went to her room and put on jeans and a jumper. They locked the house and walked down to the wet sand, as it was easier to walk along. Mike took Lauren's hand and little miss decided to walk in the middle of them so she could hold both their hands. Lauren winked at Mike, as this was the first time Sally had let a man near her. Nothing was said, but it was noticed big time!

Sally was enjoying her treat to McDonald's, was chattering away holding the floor, then something happened and she retreated into her shell. The chattering stopped and a strange quietness descended over her. Some new people had come in for a meal and they sat at the next table. They were an Asian family. Mike noticed each time the man looked their way, Sally ducked behind Lauren. It was as if she didn't want him to see her. Was she frightened? Did this bring back memories from the past? He drew Lauren's attention to the situation. "Excuse me, I'm off to the loo," said Lauren, which left Sally exposed to the man's gaze. Sally panicked: "Don't leave me here on my own, take me with you, Lauren?" she pleaded as tears ran down her cheeks. Lauren took her hand and they went to the loo together. The plot was thickening, the Asian man had definitely put fear into Sally. It almost confirmed it must have been the Asian man who visited the Stuarts that had inflicted the scars on the girls. But didn't they know this was going on? Lauren had remembered seeing him in the apartment alone with each of the girls and she did worry at the time. Oh my God, she thought, what else had he done to them? How was she ever going to find out? It wouldn't come from Sally; he must have threatened them with their lives if this was ever mentioned. The poor girls, this was an added burden on them. How could Sally ever completely mend if she could not rid herself of this fear, as this was part of the healing process? Did this mean she would never be a normal young girl ever again? As they arrived home Mike asked Sally if she enjoyed herself at McDonald's? "McDonald's food was good but ..." then she stopped. He tried to coax her to continue, but the conversation was finished, it was dead and buried. One definitely knew when they had met Sally's limits!

Lauren poured a glass of wine for herself and Mike and a soft drink for Sally. They sat and talked, then Sally decided to go to bed. "When are you going home?" she asked Mike. "He is staying the night," Lauren replied. "Why does he stay here?" "Because he is my boyfriend, I like him to stay with me," she let Sally know. "Does he sleep in your bed?" "Yes, we share my bed, why?" "Yuk" came back the reply. Once again, they couldn't hide their laughter. "One day you will meet someone you like," said Lauren hoping to push the boundaries. "It will not be a man, I will find a girlfriend like you, Lauren, someone who is kind and bossy." This brought a silence to the room. Yes, she was definitely hurting from something and it pointed to the male gender. Lauren waited until she heard Sally calling, "I'm ready, Lauren." Then she went and tucked her in with her trademark goodnight kiss. "I love you, Lauren, do you love me?" she asked. "Yes, Sally, I love you dearly. Do you know, when you love someone you share your secrets with them. They are called secrets because only the two of you know, no one else knows." "I have a secret, I'll tell you one day, but you can't tell anyone!" Sally said adamantly. And that was the end, no amount of coaxing would make her tell. Lauren knew not to push Sally for information if it was not forthcoming. She just hoped she didn't have to wait too long for her to share her secret with her. Would this unlock the heartache she was harbouring?

After settling Sally, Mike and Lauren went to bed. Lauren told Mike the conversation that had just taken place and he was saddened by what he heard. Yes, there was definitely something sinister lurking in the background and he had a suspicion it involved the Asian guy who visited the apartment. This they needed to find out, but it would probably not be through Sally. He took Lauren in his arms. He wanted to put all thoughts of Sally aside for the moment and bring Lauren a little happiness! He caressed her neck then slowly worked his way down her body. Lauren loved it when Mike was intimate with her, she longed for him to be with her, to want her, then to take her, this was the ultimate. This was the language of love! Nothing brought her as much joy as being loved by this understanding man. They shared so much in common. Most of all he loved Sally, she was part of the deal. She wondered if Sally would ever find such love, had this been stolen from her? She prayed that one day she could share these beautiful feelings with another, but was it ever going to be a happening thing? One would just have to wait and see! She looked at Mike and kissed him, then the lovers drifted off to sleep.

At some ungodly hour of the night, Lauren was woken by Sally standing at the side of her bed sobbing and tugging on the bedcovers. "Lauren, I saw him, don't leave me, take me with you." Lauren was startled. "Sally, what's happened, who did you see?" "McDonald's, that man ..." was all she could get out amid her sobs. Mike had woken and heard all this, but he didn't want his presence to interfere with what she was relating to Lauren, so he lay still.

"Come, my pet, back to bed, he can't hurt you, you are safe here with me," and she took Sally to her room and helped her into bed. She stayed with her rubbing her forehead until she dropped off to sleep.

When she made it back to her bed, Mike was waiting for her. "Lauren, do you realise those were the same words Sally used at McDonald's when you went to go to the loo? It was definitely the presence of that Asian guy that upset her. She must have gone to bed with it on her mind. I'm going to get to the bottom of this tomorrow. I'll conduct an interview with the bastard, he is in custody at the station." "Do you think he will admit to anything? I think not. He will lie to save his own skin. I have read about the cruel underworld, they are cheats and liars. I hate them, look how they can screw up innocent lives. They are cowards who prey on the vulnerable," said an upset Lauren. "They all need to be locked up for good, never to be released, why should they get a second chance at life? What if Sally never recovers? Her life has been ruined, she doesn't get a second chance!" "I know, Lauren, we are up against this every day and most of the time they are one step ahead of us. Sadly, it is always the victim that suffers, but we do our best, I know sometimes it doesn't seem enough, but this is the reality of life. You have put your life on hold to help these girls, Lauren, that is a wonderful quality to have. They need a gentle understanding person to turn to. Your contribution to their lives is the best healing process they could ever wish for. This is your 'calling', my love, it makes you happy," and with this he took her in his arms. "I'm so proud of you!"

Today was a new day. Mike had left early, he had an agenda to attend to. Sally was late out of bed, as she had had a restless night, not that she remembered any of it! She was surprised when Lauren reminded her of her antics last night. "Was Mike wild with me?" she asked. "No, of course not, he was asleep." She didn't tell her what she had said, just that she was dreaming and had come and woken her up. What she and Mike had witnessed was another piece of the puzzle!

After breakfast, they decided to take a walk along the beach and take in the healthy salt air. A big distance had been covered when they decided to take a rest in the sand dunes. As they were lying on their backs, picking forms out of the clouds, Lauren kept hearing whimpering. "Do you hear anything, Sally?" She listened and yes, it was still there. Lauren stood up and went to see where it was coming from. Less than one hundred yards further on, there lying curled up among the tussocks was a young girl. She was only partly dressed — her jeans were intact, but she was bare from the waist up. What had happened to this poor soul? Her top was lying a few feet away. Other than that there was nothing — no bag, no shoes. Who was this girl?

Sally had got up and come over, and stood there next to Lauren in bewilderment. "Lauren, we have to bring her home with us, she has no one. We can't leave her here, someone might hurt her," she sobbed. She went over to her and held her hand, but she never stirred. Lauren picked up her top and had a look around for anything else that might relate to her, but there was nothing. She put it over her, so as to cover her nakedness, but there was nothing of her. Her feminine shape had all but disappeared, she was just skin and bone. Then she told Sally they would sit and wait until she came around, or someone came for her.

An hour had passed and all that came from her was the odd whimper that escaped every so often. This is what had drawn them to her. Sally sat with tears streaming down her face. Was this what she looked like when Lauren found her? she wondered. How sad! "Wake up, little girl, we will look after you," she pleaded as she shook her limp body. The sound of voices was enough to make her aware that someone was there. "Please help me?" she sobbed. "Lauren will help you, she helped me," Sally assured her. She tried to sit up, but fell down again. "What is wrong with her, Lauren?" asked Sally. Lauren knew what was wrong, it was there in her eyes. She had the same look as Sally when they first met. "She has been drugged, like you were. We will wait until she can walk, then we will take her home with us." "That's a good idea, Lauren," agreed Sally. They sat for ages before the girl fully found her feet. She knew nothing, not even her name or how she came to be there. Suddenly she realised she was half-naked then started to panic, "Why am I like this, where is my top?" she called out. Lauren went to her and helped her put it on, she was in tears. They helped her along the beach, propping her up, as she was in pain. Lauren was watching to see how Sally was coping. She couldn't get over how sympathetic she was towards this stranger. She wondered if Sally felt a little jealous, but it was not showing thus far.

As they made their way down the beach they were disturbed by a young man. "What are you doing with my girlfriend?" and he rushed up to the young stranger and tried to pull her free. "Come with me, Maddie, do as you're told," but she tried to fend him off, telling him to leave her alone. Then an angry Sally retaliated. She lashed out at him and kicked him in the shins, yelling at him to leave her friend alone. With this warning he took off. "Thank you," whispered the young girl. Lauren and Sally half carried her home, where they took her to the spare room and lay her on the bed. All she wanted was to be left alone until the effects of the drugs wore off, so Lauren brought over a rug and tucked her in. She closed the door and went to find Sally. She wanted to thank her for being so caring. "I'm proud of you, Sally, that was kind of you to care for and protect a complete stranger." "But Lauren, you did that for me," was her response. Lauren took her in her arms and held her. "You are the best thing that has happened to me, you have turned my life around. I want to be here for young girls like yourself who need help, it is my calling." "I love you, bossy Lauren," and they both laughed.

The whole afternoon slipped by and still no sign of the stranger. As tea time approached, Lauren became worried so went into the room. The young girl was as Lauren had left her, but her breathing was shallow and she looked pale. She felt her and she was cold and sweaty. It was time to dial for an ambulance, as she looked like she had lapsed into a coma. She called to Sally who rushed in and when she saw the girl, she realised that something was wrong. "She's not dead, is she, Lauren?" "Not yet, but she is very sick. Hold her hand so she knows someone is with her." Lauren called the ambulance again to see how far away it was, as she was afraid it might arrive too late. A few minutes later it arrived and in rushed the paramedics with an oxygen mask and a cylinder. After examining her and putting the mask on her, they told Lauren she was in a coma. Whatever she had taken had poisoned her system causing it to slowly shut down. "Do you know what she has taken?" they asked. Lauren explained the situation. She knew nothing so was of no help. They lifted her onto the stretcher and wheeled her out to the ambulance. "My name is Lauren, please let us know how she is," she requested. "Does she have a name?" the ambulance men called. "I think it is Maddie," replied Lauren.

# 9

# Mike's quest to find the truth

Mike held a meeting with his superiors and lay it on the table, all that had been happening at Lauren's home, the state of Sally, her fears and what they thought she had endured — and by whom! He asked for permission to try to extract the truth from the Asian guy, who was held in one of their cells at the station. This he was granted. It was arranged for the prisoner to be taken to the interview room at two o'clock, where Mike would attempt to hound him until he told the truth. Not that he held out much hope that he would talk, but he would try to get justice for Sally. He had to find out how the girls had suffered and why. He sat at the desk waiting for the guards to bring him in. He would be handcuffed for the interview and the guards would be outside the door. The cameras and speakers were switched on.

Within a few minutes the door opened and in walked the Asian man. Mike told him to be seated. "What is your name and where are you from?" were the first questions. He said his name was Hiroshi and he was born in Japan, but had moved to China as a young man, before coming to Australia. "What do you work at here in Australia?" Mike asked. "I came to Australia and started a business of importing goods from China, to sell to retailers." "Is that how you became involved in drug dealing?" He denied anything about being involved with drugs. "But I caught you in the Stuarts' apartment when I arrested them," Mike told him. He said he was just visiting, he had only just met them through church. "Have you visited them often?" He told Mike he had only just met them and this was his first visit. "You can truthfully tell me you had never been to their apartment before we arrested them?" He swore he was telling the truth. "Now that is a certain lie, Hiroshi. I saw you in that unit one morning, counting cash that was lying in bundles on the bench-top." "No, no, not me!" he said. "Did you ever see anyone else there when you visited?" "No, only the Stuarts," he answered. "What about the young girls, did you see them there?" He denied he has seen any young girls during his visits.

Now he had come unstuck, because he originally said that was his first visit, now he was saying there no young girls there when he visited. "You are lying, Mr Hiroshi, you did see the young girls, you were in the apartment alone with each girl at different times." He vehemently denied these accusations. "The next question, what did you do to those girls?" asked Mike. "What do you mean?" "You inflicted pain on them. What did you do?" His eyes diverted away from Mike, he could not look him in the eye, even to lie. This was enough to make Mike think he did indeed hurt the girls. "Did you know the first young girl drowned? Her body was found washed up on the rocks in a nearby bay. The postmortem showed drugs in her system and raw scars on her back and buttocks. How did they get there?" "I don't know what you are talking about," he answered. With this Mike stood up and banged his fist on the table. "We have two girls who were cruelly treated by you, you hurt them. For the last time, what did you do to them? They both had the same scars on their bodies. Thank God one survived. I am going to bring her to the station to identify you. Not only will you go down for dealing in drugs, but you will go down for cruelty, for which you will be handed a lengthy prison sentence." Silence reigned. Mr Hiroshi was not in the least bit frightened of the girls, as they knew what would happen if they said anything. He had silenced them. "I will get you in the end, mark my words, these girls will suffer no longer. You are a marked man. Think about this overnight, I will see you tomorrow, now get the hell out of here." Mike banged on the door for the guards to take him back to his cell. He didn't get any truths from him, but hopefully as he thought about it overnight, he might find it in his heart to own up to what he had done to the girls. He was cornered, there was no way out!

Mike had also arranged with his superiors to speak with the Stuarts. He would question them separately and see what stories they came up with. First, he would question Mrs Stuart. She was shown into the interview room and was asked to sit down. "Now, Mrs Stuart, how did you become involved in the drug scene?" asked Mike. She told him she knew nothing about drugs. "You never found any evidence in our apartment when you did the search," she fired back. "No, we didn't, and the reason being they were gotten rid of the night before. We know of your movements: when the parcels were delivered, the drugs were offloaded the same night, may I add, by your fake daughter who was your drug mule." "What do you mean? She was my daughter, I wouldn't let her be involved with drugs." "Oh, is that so? What happened when she went missing and didn't come back? You never reported her missing." "What do you mean?" she asked.

"Do you know why she never came back? Her backpack was found washed up on the beach one morning. It was still full of drugs; the delivery had not been made. The next morning during a helicopter search her body was found washed up on the rocks. It was taken to the mortuary for a postmortem and it was found she had drugs in her system. Did you know this, Mrs Stuart?" The look of disbelief on her face told Mike she knew nothing about this, she was shaking. "Also, on the body were raw scars, they were on her back and buttocks. What did you and your husband do to those girls?" "What do you mean, what scars? I know nothing about these." She was in shock, it was genuine shock. Suddenly things started going through her mind. Did her husband hurt the girls when she went out? Surely not. If not, how did the scars get there? Her mind was in a whirl: one girl drowned, what happened to the other one? She was too afraid to ask. "Well, either you, your husband, or Mr Hiroshi tortured those poor girls. Thank God one of them has survived, but she is so traumatised she is unable to talk about what happened. But the truth will come out and someone will be severely punished for this." Tears ran down Mrs Stuart's face. No, she definitely did not know anything about the torture of the girls. "It is sad to think both those girls went to the church for help and you used them as drug mules, feeding them up on drugs to carry out your dirty work, when they were entrusted in your care to be nurtured. You and your husband will suffer for this grave injustice that you have caused these girls. Two young lives have been ruined. I am thinking of bringing the parents of your so-called daughter, the girl that drowned, into the station, just so they can see who virtually murdered her, their only child. They are devastated. Now get out of here and think about the heartache you have caused. May you suffer the same!" Mike banged on the door for her to be taken away.

He didn't know if by speaking to Mr Stuart, he was going to learn any more than what he already knew. Perhaps he could frighten him into spilling on Mr Hiroshi. Yes, he would talk to him and see what came out of it. He was brought into the interview room. "Sit down, Mr Stuart. I will start with a most serious question. What did you do to those young girls to inflict the scars on their back and buttocks?" "What do you mean?" he asked. Mike explained about the scars and asked what he had done to the girls. There was a shocked look on his face, which told Mike that he had nothing to do with it. "Well, Mr Hiroshi denied hurting the girls, so did your wife, so that only leaves you. This is a serious offence and will be dealt with accordingly. Mr Stuart sat dumbfounded, he knew nothing of this. "Did you know why the young girl you registered as your daughter never came back? She walked into the sea and drowned. Her backpack was found washed up on the beach in front of your apartment and still contained the drugs. The drop-off was not performed. You are in serious trouble. If you didn't hurt the girls, then who did?" Mr Stuart asked about the scars and when Mike said they were round and had penetrated the skin, he knew immediately who it was. "Mr Hiroshi was a smoker, would he have done it with a cigarette? Oh my God, that is horrible. I promise I didn't know about this," he stated. Mike was upset. The interview was called to an end and the guards were summoned to take Mr Stuart back to his cell.

Yes, as he suspected, they were definitely burns, but to be burnt by a cigarette, no wonder Sally couldn't talk about it. Then to see that Asian man at McDonald's must have brought it all back to her. No wonder she was frightened. What a bastard. Mr Hiroshi would go down hard for the cruelty he had inflicted on these girls, but the Stuarts would also suffer, as they were meant to be their guardians. The seedy underworld of drugs extended to cruelty and abandonment, a life was worth nothing, it was easily replaced by another and on it went. Such a sad environment to be dragged into!

That night Mike couldn't get to sleep, he was still reeling from the interviews. None of this had affected him before. It wasn't that he didn't care, but since he had met Lauren and become involved with Sally, it had become a personal matter, one that had resonated in his heart. He had a better understanding of why people were so distraught when he had to be the bearer of bad news to bereaved families. Now he felt Sally had become a member of his and Lauren's family. Why am I thinking like this? he asked himself. It was only then that he faced the reality of his love for Lauren and his feelings for Sally. They were a package never to be separated. He loved that Lauren had taken her in and cared for her. He could see all this being part of his life. One that he had been searching for, but never found ... until now!

This morning Mike was back in the interview room with Mr Hiroshi. Today he meant business, as last night his life had been sorted and now he looked on Sally as his own. How would he feel? Very angry, in fact bloody angry! "Right, I am after the truth, that is all I want. We know you hurt the girls, what did you do to them?" asked Mike. "I know nothing about the girls." He was in denial. This riled Mike and he couldn't restrain himself any longer. He stood up and hit the table with his fist. He was angry. "This is your last chance to tell the truth. What happened to those girls?" Suddenly Mr Hiroshi became alarmed. He looked around, but there was no escaping, he was in this room with a very angry man. But would he own up? Never! Denial was better than owning up, he had learnt this in the drug underworld. Owning up meant sudden death, denying was survival, it was tough out there! Mike could see this was a closed case, but how were they ever going to find out what had happened? It was apparent that the girls had been burnt by cigarettes, but was that all that had happened to them, or was there hurt elsewhere? It was tearing him apart. Only two people knew what really happened: Sally, who was unwilling to talk of her horror, and Mr Hiroshi, who was in denial, but who was the perpetrator. One of them would have to talk ... but who? All interviews were called to an end.

# 10

# A new arrival at Lauren's home

Meanwhile back at Lauren's home, she and Sally were waiting for news on Maddie. They had talked until late last night, both worried that she wasn't going to be alive today. Lauren still couldn't get over how caring and concerned Sally was towards Maddie, it warmed her heart to see these feelings being expressed. Suddenly the phone rang, it was the hospital wanting to know if Lauren could come down. A young girl called Maddie was asking for someone to be with her and the ambulance driver had given them Lauren's name. "Yes, I'm on my way now," she told them. "Come on, Sally, Maddie is asking for us." They hurried to the car as they were both anxious to see her. When they arrived at the hospital it brought back sad memories for Sally, but she had come a long way since then. They were taken to the locked door that had been Sally's home for several weeks. She took Lauren's hand, as she needed that feeling of security. The door was unlocked and they were shown to Maddie's bed.

She looked frightened and her eyes were darting from

side to side as if she was trying to escape from something. Before Lauren got a chance to speak, Sally had rushed to her. "Hello, Maddie, remember me and Lauren? We found you in the sand dunes," and as she was saying this, she took Maddie's hand. Lauren looked at her, this was Sally all over again, these poor girls, why were they preyed upon? "How are you feeling today?" she asked. "I feel awful." "You will feel like this for a few days but you will get better. Sally will be able to tell you, as this was her bed when she was sick." "You will get better, Maddie. I was sick too, but look at me, Lauren rescued me, I know she will rescue you, won't you, Lauren?" asked Sally. "Do you have family who can care for you?" asked Lauren. "Not anyone who cares, no one wants me. I'm not a good girl," she sobbed. Lauren asked her how old she was. "I'm seventeen, I left home when I was sixteen with my boyfriend." "Was that him on the beach yesterday, the one who tried to take you away?" she asked. "Yes, but he got me on drugs so he could sell me for money. Please don't let him take me away, I don't want to go there again," she pleaded. "We will look after you, Maddie. Lauren and I will bring you to our home, won't we, Lauren?" This brought a smile to Lauren; now her house had become their home. "Yes, when you are well enough to leave hospital, you can come and stay with us."

Was this the start of her dream, to make a home for needy girls? Was she ready for another? Because Sally was happy about it, that was good enough for Lauren. She would have to share Lauren's time with another. Now it would be a three-way share, not forgetting Mike! As they were leaving, the nurse asked for Lauren to come and speak with the doctor, as she had some sad news for her. "While we had Maddie sedated, we found she had been abused multiple times and there was damage done internally, so she is going to need an operation. This will leave her unable to have children of her own. She is badly bruised from her waist down. We have told her we have to operate, but we haven't told her of the consequences. That will have to come later, as we feel she has suffered enough." Lauren was in shock, what terrible news for anyone to have to hear. She agreed it would be too much for her to take in at the moment, but one day she would have to be told. How would she take this?

Tonight, Mike was coming to stay for a couple of days as he had time off. He had put a lot of thought in lately on his future, and Lauren was definitely part of it. He loved her company and he knew Sally was always going to be part of any arrangement he made with her. He wanted to tell Lauren about his interviews with Mr Hiroshi and the Stuarts, of which the outcome was disappointing to say the least. From these talks, the only conclusion he had come to was how the scars got on Sally's back and buttocks. But this was not by admission from anyone! But there was still no evidence if Sally had been sexually abused. This is what they needed to know at this stage, but who was going to be forthcoming with this information?

Where did Lance fit into the picture? The police commissioner had stood him down, and he was held in custody at this point in time. He had perverted the course of justice by informing the criminals that their apartment had been bugged. Very little conversation had been discussed that was of any consequence to help the police with their investigation. There was periodic sobbing heard, this would have been from the girls, as they were being hurt. Thank goodness all the phone calls from reception regarding the parcel deliveries had been recorded, so this was something to start with, but they did not have a strong case. It would all be down to Mike, Lauren and Sally to give evidence against the Stuarts and Mr Hiroshi in court. Not that they knew of this at this point in time.

Lauren was happy when Mike arrived as she had missed him, even more so now that they were lovers. Sally had come around to thinking he was okay, as he seemed to make Lauren happy. She was a little apprehensive as to why she would let him sleep with her in her bed. She would never share her bed with a man, they were not very nice people. Well, the ones she knew weren't. Even her father hit her mother and that was why Sally ran away, because her mother was always crying. But Mike didn't seem to hurt Lauren, she was happy when he was near her. She couldn't understand how he could make her so happy? Sally had a mixed-up mind about men, she only knew them as being cruel and who hurt women and girls. This behaviour was all she had seen in her life thus far, so of course she didn't have a good understanding of them. Even Maddie didn't want to see her boyfriend again, as he had started her on drugs. Sally's opinion of men was very low. Would this ever change, was it too late, was the damage permanent?

While Mike opened a bottle of wine, Lauren put some nibbles together, then they went out onto the patio to soak up some of the late afternoon sun. Lauren had on a sun frock and was bare-footed so she was in relax mode. Sally was pottering away in the spare bedroom as she was getting it organised for Maddie. Next time she visited, she would ask Maddie what her favourite colour was, then she and Lauren would paint her room. She decided to let Mike and Lauren have a little time on their own. Mike pulled up his chair close to Lauren and they had a cheer, then sipped their wine. He told her about the interviews, and that it was almost certain that it was the Asian man who had inflicted the scars on the girls, by burning them with a cigarette. Lauren was shocked to hear this and tears fell from her eyes as Mike relayed this to her. How could anyone be so cruel? At this stage they still did not know if Sally had been sexually abused! He decided not to tell her about having to appear in court to give evidence, as her tears prevented him from speaking further on the subject.

He got up from his chair and came over to Lauren and knelt in front of her, then took something out of his pocket. "Lauren, I love you dearly. Will you marry me?" and he took her hand and slipped a ring on her finger. This was a shock, she didn't see this coming, what a wonderful surprise! "Oh Mike, yes, yes yes!" she said in excitement. She had secretly hoped one day Mike would love her, as she loved him, but to be his wife, this was beyond her wildest dreams. But what of Sally and now Maddie? It was only then she realised she hadn't told him about Maddie. Would this make him change his mind? All this aside, she jumped up out of her chair into his waiting arms. She looked at the ring, it was exquisite, just what she would have chosen for herself! With all this excitement Sally came rushing in to see what all the commotion was about. "Mike has asked me to marry him, isn't that wonderful, Sally?" "But you have me and Maddie to look after, you can't look after him too? That will be too much for you, Lauren," she said in earnest. If Mike hadn't understood Sally's wit, he would have been hurt by these remarks, but all it brought was laughter. "Who is Maddie?" he asked, knowing that he was going to be told by Sally. "I will tell him, Lauren. We found another girl who needs Lauren and me to look after her, she is in hospital at the moment."

Lauren told Mike they would talk about it later, as this was a cherished moment, one to enjoy. They came inside and sat on the settee together with their arms around each other.

Lauren could not have been happier. She had met the man of her dreams, someone who understood her concern for abused girls and her dedication to helping them. He would have to share his life with more than just Lauren. Perhaps she should have asked him, before accepting his proposal. Now was probably the time to mention about Maddie and see how he felt. "Mike, yesterday Sally and I found a young girl half-dressed lying in the sand dunes. She was drugged and didn't know what had happened to her. She was naked from the waist up, her top was lying away from her." Then Lauren told him what had happened, and about the young guy who tried to take her away, but Sally frightened him off. Her name was Maddie. Then she continued with what followed next and how she came to be in hospital. "When she comes out of hospital, I want her to come here so I can look after her. Sally likes her and wants to help care for her. I just want you to understand this is my calling. If it is not acceptable to you, then all we can be is lovers. I love you, Mike, but I cannot let go of my promise to myself to care for these girls. My heart was deeply wounded when the first young girl drowned. I want to try to prevent it ever happening again. Can you accept me on these terms?" "That's what I love most about you, Lauren, your caring nature. I don't like seeing these young girls abused and, to be truthful, I have seen too many of them disappear never to be found. Some parents must live in absolute agony not knowing what has happened to their kids. I will support you all the way. It won't be easy, but we will work it out together," he assured her. This made Lauren very happy to know she could have the most important things in her life, she didn't have to choose. It would have been totally different if she was still with Scott — it would have been his way or no way! Meeting Mike was a blessing sent to her from someone who believed in her, someone who was looking out for her and put her on a new path for which she had to follow. It was a path that came direct from her heart.

"Lauren, when is tea ready? Mike and I are hungry, aren't we, Mike?" asked Sally. She was sick of all this kerfuffle about being engaged, as there were more important things to think about ... such as food. "We will order a pizza, Lauren is not cooking tonight," Mike told Sally, as he took the top off another bottle of wine. It was a night of celebration! He then rang for a pizza delivery. Sally sat and watched. It was nice to see Lauren so happy, but she couldn't understand why. Lauren was enjoying the extra glass of wine, why not, this was the day her lover had asked her to marry him, it was special. As they were celebrating, Sally had walked over to the gate, opened it and walked out onto the beach. She had seen someone she thought she knew — he had been watching the property. It was all too much for her, being the nosy person she was, she had to find out who it was.

As she got closer, she recognised him as the guy she had argued with yesterday, over Maddie. "What are you doing spying on us?" she asked him. "Where is Maddie?" "She is in hospital. Don't you ever come near her again, she hates you," she let him know. "She will come back to me, just you wait and see." "No, I won't let her, she told me you hurt her, we don't like men. She is going to get better so you stay away!" Sally warned him. Then she heard Lauren calling for her to come and have something to eat. Her passing words to him: "I won't tell you again, don't come near her ever again or I will deal to you." "You think you are tough, we will see about that!" he yelled at her. When she came back inside the gate Lauren asked her who she was talking to. "Oh, just someone I know." This worried her so she was persistent with her questioning. "If you must know it was Maddie's boyfriend. I told him not to come near her again or I would deal to him." Now it was time for Mike to step in. "Sally, don't try to be brave, you stay away from him. If he is into drugs, he will have mates. Don't go on the beach again without Lauren or myself, do you understand?" "Yes, bossy Mike." Now we had a bossy Lauren and a bossy Mike. This made Lauren smile, it was as if this was an affectionate word, coming from Sally's mouth.

Sally was sick of all the happiness that was going on between Lauren and Mike, it was time for her to go to bed. She couldn't wait for Maddie to come and live with them, then she would have a new friend. The two lovers celebrated well into the night, well, most of the night. Their bed became the hottest place in town. Lauren was so happy she had met Mike, amid all the chaos that was going on in her life. In the morning they were woken by Sally standing at the bedroom door. "Get out of Lauren's bed, Mike, there are some guys watching our house." "Go, Sally, so he can get dressed!" said Lauren as she was still standing there. "Don't be bossy Lauren," she said as she left the room. Mike threw on his clothes and went and had a look out the lounge window, and yes, there were several young men standing just a few metres from their fence. He made his way towards them. "What are you doing hanging around here? Now clear off!" he yelled at them. Then he recognised one of the guys, as he had been involved with him in the past. He was a real bad egg. He made his way inside and asked Sally which was the guy involved with Maddie. When she pointed him out, yes, that was the bad one. He was known to the police for dealing in drugs. How the hell did she get mixed up with him? He would sell his own grandmother. He feared for Maddie. Had he used her as a sex slave to get money to feed his habit? Then he remembered Lauren had said she and Sally had found her half-naked in the sand dunes, totally out to it. The bastard, he thought, he would keep his eye on him. Then he worried, would Lauren and Sally be safe here? What would happen when Maddie arrived? The first sign of trouble he would put the house under police surveillance, but he elected not to mention this, as he didn't want to cause any undue panic.

Mike had left this morning, as he had an undercover job that would take him away for a number of days. Just how many, he didn't know. The hospital had rung to say Maddie had had her operation and needed to be in a home environment, as she was not responding as well as they would have liked. She was still on heavy medication, but if Lauren thought she could look after her, they would be most grateful. There was no hesitation on her behalf, so she arranged to pick her up later that afternoon. But first she wanted to visit the Blue Water Apartments and see how Anna was faring with her new boss! She hadn't spoken with her since she had left and felt terrible about this, as they got on so well together. But what of Sally, would she remember her past there? Perhaps she could ask her to stay in the car, she wouldn't be long. As they pulled up outside the apartment block and Lauren stopped the car, Sally spoke: "I'm not getting out here, can I stay in the car, Lauren? I don't want to go in there again. I feel safer in the car." Lauren told her she wouldn't be long, she just wanted to talk to Anna. "Okay, Lauren, but don't talk too long because I'm in the car on my own," was Sally's response. She thought she would ask Anna to come outside where she could talk and see the car. As she made her way to reception, Anna was busy taking bookings over the phone. When Lauren gave a little cough, she looked up but could not hold Lauren's gaze. Instead her eyes diverted in another direction. What's going on here? she thought. Then Scott appeared. "Hi ,Lauren, how is everything in your life?" he asked. "Fine, thank you, Scott. I've just popped in to tell Anna that Mike and I are engaged." He offered Lauren his congratulations, then disappeared. "Anna, don't tell me my worst fear, are you and Scott an item? Surely not." "Yes, I have moved in with him," she answered and she hung her head, unable to look at Lauren. "I am so disappointed in you, he will trap you, but I did warn you, Anna. I hope it all goes well for you," and with these passing words, she left. Silly Anna, she thought, but like myself she wouldn't listen, neither would Lucy. These were lovestruck girls, who all knew best. Would there be another victim, or was it going to end here? As she walked to her car, she hoped she would never have to say to Anna 'I told you so!'

Now it was time to go to the hospital and pick up Maddie. Sally was excited, she was going to have a new friend. When they arrived at the hospital, they were taken to an office so the nurse could explain what medication Maddie was on and how it had to be administered. She had not settled down in the hospital, as none of the nurses could help her, as she wouldn't let them near her. The nurse told Lauren she was badly bruised from the waist down, due to having been abused at the hands of some very rough men.

They were hoping Lauren could win her over and administer the relevant ointments to where they were needed. This brought tears to both Lauren and Sally. Would she ever be able to find out who treated her so badly? Did she even know, if she was drugged, would she have felt this hurt? So many unanswered questions, but if there were no answers then perhaps her memory had erased all the horrible past from her mind.

Maddie was brought out by a nurse. There was just her, nothing else, no luggage accompanied her, she came with nothing, just as Sally had. She smiled in recognition of Lauren and Sally. Sally walked up to her and took her hand. "We are taking you to our home, we will look after you." Lauren smiled, there was that statement again, 'our home'. It was comforting to know she looked upon it as her home. Hopefully Maddie would feel the same way after she had settled in. The hospital staff were there to wave goodbye to Maddie. They knew she needed one-on-one care, something they couldn't give her. She was to be brought back in a fortnight for a check-up to see if everything was healing as it should be. They wished Lauren the best of luck, as they knew it was going to be a sad path to travel, but she had travelled it before with Sally and the end results were worth the journey! Sally climbed into the back seat with Maddie, all the time never letting go of her hand. This brought tears to Lauren's eyes, as she knew Sally had been there, so probably understood more than anyone else how it felt. These girls both needed to be comforted and nurtured in the initial stages of their recovery. As they drove home and pulled up in Lauren's drive, Maddie asked Sally, "Have I been here before?" "Yes, Maddie, Lauren and I brought you here, then you were taken away in the ambulance. This is your new home. You can pick a colour for your bedroom, then we can both paint it. Lauren will pay for the paint!" They walked into the house and Maddie explored all the rooms. "Which room would you like?" Sally asked her. She picked the one next to Sally's. "That's a good choice, now we can be neighbours." Lauren listened to these young girls, and their lack of education meant, mentally they were well below their age group. But they were just starting to rebuild their lives from scratch again, as their brains had been affected by the drugs. First, they would have to learn the basic life skills before anything else.

Lauren asked Maddie what her favourite foods were, so she would know what to cook for her. It was better to start them eating properly again on foods they enjoyed. But, like Sally, she had no particular likes, as her taste buds had been altered and all food tasted similar. She decided to start the evening meal with a platter of meat and vegetables, then she could see what she was choosing to eat. It was sad how drugs took away their eating pleasures and that they were just functioning to stay alive. All they needed was one fix followed by the next, so food was bypassed. No wonder they ended up skinny, scrawny girls, their female attributes almost non-existent and their hair straggly and unhealthy. Lauren noticed Sally was starting to develop and her breasts were filling out, everything was slowly coming back to normal, so this was a promising sign. Once the drugs were flushed through their system and the toxins got rid of, they began their journey to recovery. Lauren understood they would never be completely normal, but if she could get them as near to normal as possible, then she had achieved all she could hope for.

She watched Maddie picking at the food. She was hesitant about everything, but she did manage to put a little away. It was a start and she wouldn't push her. She would come around in her own time. After they finished eating, Lauren made them clear up and wash the dishes. "That's bossy Lauren!" she told Maddie in a semi-whisper, knowing that it would be heard. Lauren went and sat on the settee to see if Maddie would come and sit beside her. "Move over, Lauren, make room for Maddie and me, we both need a cuddle," and with this she had a girl on each side. She put an arm around each one and they moved closer to her. Sally had turned into a loving being and Lauren was hoping Maddie would be the same. She was sure Sally would train her well in that direction. "Right, Maddie, what colour do you want your room painted?" she asked. "I like blue," she replied. "But there are lots of blues, which blue?" and Lauren went away and brought back a colour chart, then told her to pick the blue she liked. Once it was all sorted, Sally handed out instructions for Lauren to buy the paint. She had turned into the proper little organiser.

When it came to night-time, Lauren asked Maddie when she would like to have a shower, morning or night. She didn't seem very forthcoming with an answer so she didn't push it tonight. They went through the medications as she had a heavy dosage to take before she went to bed. Lauren didn't know if Maddie would sleep right through the night or if it would mean a broken sleep for her. Time would tell, but she would be prepared! The girls went to their rooms. Sally had given Maddie a pair of her pyjamas until they went shopping. Lauren heard laughter coming from Sally's room, they seemed to be getting on well together. Then the nightly call from Sally, "Lauren, I'm ready!" This was the sign for Lauren to come and tuck her in and for her goodnight cuddle. As she left Sally's room she peeped in Maddie's room. "Can I come in?" she asked. "Yes, Lauren," came a whisper. She went and sat on Maddie's bed and reached for her hand. "I hope you will be happy here with us. I want to help you get off the drugs and live a happy life. We can do it together, Maddie. Look at Sally, she was just like you, now she is well on her way to recovery. Give me a cuddle, that's what we do here in this home," and the tears started. Maddie nestled into Lauren and sobbed. She felt lost and loved at the same time, someone actually cared for her! Lauren tucked her in and gave her a goodnight hug. "If you need me during the night, just call I'll be here for you," Lauren whispered to her.

Lauren was tired as she climbed into bed. It had been another full day and with each day came hope. Her heart was filled with compassion for these two girls. She could see Maddie was deeply distressed. From what she had worked out thus far, her boyfriend had fed her drugs then sold her body to whoever. As long as he received payment, then he could feed his habit. This was pitiful, it was a form of prostitution. What would have been going through that poor girl's mind? Would she ever forgive the male species, did she even know what was happening to her at the time? The hospital said she was badly bruised below the waist, she was used and abused. She hoped one day Maddie would be able to tell her what had happened, but then perhaps, she might never want to talk about it. Just as she was about to drop off to sleep, she heard her screaming so she jumped out of bed and ran to her room. She was thrashing about in the bed as if she was trying to fend someone off her. "It's okay, Maddie, it's Lauren, no one is going to hurt you, you are safe here with me," and on hearing Lauren's voice she calmed down. Lauren lay on her bed and rubbed her forehead, all the time whispering to her that she was safe. Her sobs lessened until they were no more. Lauren pulled some covers over her and slept the rest of the night on her bed. Just for Maddie to have someone near gave her the security she needed.

When Lauren woke in the morning, she could hear the shower going and Maddie was gone. She lay there, but her eyes wouldn't stay open as she was still tired. Maddie came back into the room wrapped in a towel and saw Lauren was still asleep so she turned her back and dropped the towel to get dressed. At that moment Lauren stirred and got the shock of her life to see how badly bruised Maddie's body was. She wouldn't let on, as she didn't want to lose her trust, or for her to feel embarrassed about it, but it was enough to produce tears of sympathy for this lost soul. What she must have endured ... hell! Hopefully she was that drugged she felt nothing! Lauren waited until Maddie was dressed and left the room before she fully stirred. The smell of toast wafted up the hallway and when Lauren arrived in the kitchen, the two girls were having breakfast.

Just as they were getting ready to go to town, a car pulled up at Lauren's home. It was the parents of the drowned girl. They had come to see how Lauren was managing and also to see how Sally was progressing. Lauren invited them in and made them a cup of tea and they all sat around the table. They couldn't get over the difference in Sally, she was bright and happy. Why couldn't their daughter have been saved? but they were grateful that one of the girls had survived. They thought of their daughter every day, and wanted to know when the Stuarts were appearing in court, as they wanted to be there each day and watch that justice was done. Maddie went outside and they watched her standing by the fence. Lauren explained what they thought had happened to her, but as yet she hadn't spoken of her ordeal. They couldn't believe that there were so many girls out there being taken advantage of, and so young! "You are a godsend to these girls, Lauren, we can't thank you enough. It didn't help us, but it will help other parents, they won't have to suffer as we have." Lauren thought back to Sally's family — her mother never bothered to get back in touch again, so she didn't know if Sally was alive or dead, and here in this room were parents who missed their only child every day. Where was the justice in this? There wasn't any!

As they were talking, Lauren noticed a guy making his way towards the fence, then she recognised him as Maddie's boyfriend. She waited to see what would happen, how Maddie would react. She just stood as if she was rooted to the ground, then he suddenly lunged at her and grabbed her by her hair. Lauren jumped up and ran to her rescue, followed closely by Sally. "Take your hands off her, you coward!" she yelled. He kept hold of her hair, and she just stood like a statue and never uttered a word. As Lauren approached, he let Maddie go and took off, yelling to her, "I'll get you, bitch!" She took Maddie in her arms, she was trembling, but not a word came from her mouth. "Maddie, speak to me?" begged Lauren, but she was so afraid, nothing would come out. By this time the visitors had rushed out into the yard. They had witnessed this gross act of cruelty on this young girl, rendering her silent. The husband took his wife in his arms and they both cried together. Is this what their daughter had suffered? Lauren took Maddie inside to her bedroom and lay her on the bed and put a cover over her. Perhaps she didn't want to talk at the moment; she would leave her and come back shortly. Everyone was disgusted with what they had seen. "Lauren, do you think it is safe for you and the girls to live here?

Will he come back?" asked the visitors. "My fiancé is an undercover detective with the drug squad, he will sort him out. This is why I must help these young girls, they need protection from these lowlifes. They are drop-outs preying on the vulnerable, fancy selling someone else's body to feed a habit, that is disgusting, a young girl used as a prostitute. Drugs are evil, I fear them, but more than that, I fear the people who distribute them."

Lauren noticed Sally was missing, so she went to Maddie's room and there she was, lying on the bed with her arms around her, protecting her. Lauren went back to her visitors and apologised: "I'm sorry you had to witness this today." "You are so brave, Lauren. We have come with some more money for you, so the girls can be given a second chance at life. You must continue with this project." They didn't want other families to suffer as they were doing, but to think Sally's family didn't care and as yet Maddie hadn't discussed her family. If only life was this simple, but it was far more complicated. A cheque was handed to Lauren, and she couldn't believe how much it was for — it would keep them going for the rest of the year. The kindness of these people resonated in Lauren's heart, but she knew they wanted her to continue with her good work, so she needed money to survive and this was their contribution. Life was sad for some people, and it certainly wasn't the same for everyone. Out there was an uneven playing field.

After the visitors left, Lauren went to see how Maddie was. Sally had comforted her and they were both getting ready to go shopping. She was still a little subdued but Sally would soon sort this out, she had a way with her that seemed to overcome any obstacles. She was the ultimate peacemaker if you didn't get offended easily. As young as she was in her ways, she was like a breath of fresh air. Lauren was coming around to understanding her way of thinking. Sometimes it wasn't logic, but the mending process was still in its early stages. She often wondered if she would ever be completely normal. One would just have to be patient and see what unfolded! At the moment she still had to be nurtured and cared for. She had no concept of money and where it came from. All she knew was that Lauren would pay for everything. Lauren felt it was too soon to introduce things outside of Sally's own thinking at the moment, as her brain was still mending. Then she hoped logic would return, but who knew what lay ahead?

# 11

# Secrets shared

Lauren wanted Maddie to choose what clothes she liked to wear, but she appeared lost. Her sense of self-worth was zero and she seemed to have lost her grasp on life. She couldn't make her own decisions, she had no idea what she even liked. This brought tears to Lauren's eyes, as she just stood and looked at the racks of clothes unable to decide on anything. Why is she like this? she wondered, not realising the effect the drugs had taken on her life. They had stripped her of all reasoning and decision-making, and she was just a child again who needed guidance. "Sally, you help Maddie choose what you think she would look nice in," prompted Lauren. Sally took Maddie's hand and they looked through the racks of clothes. It wasn't hard for Sally to buy things, as Lauren always paid! After an hour they had put together a bit of a wardrobe and Maddie seemed happy. Then it was on to a sleepwear and underwear shop. Sally knew where all the knickers were, so she was in charge! She picked out all the pretty ones and Maddie trailed behind. Maddie didn't need a bra at the moment as she was just skin and bone, but hopefully, like Sally, once she was on the road to recovery, she would start to get her feminine features back again. Next it was on to the shoe shop, Sally's favourite shop. Lauren was hoping Maddie was not as keen on shoes as Sally was — she remembered the mess she left behind last visit. "Come on, Maddie, try everything on, it is such fun," said Sally, with all the encouragement in the world. Poor Maddie, she was bewildered as Sally brought shoes from all directions for her to try on. Lauren had to step in and tell Sally to let Maddie try on what she liked. Thank goodness that is all over, Lauren thought to herself as they left the shop with four pair of shoes. Sally suggested they stop off at McDonald's and get a hamburger to take away and eat in the park. Everyone agreed.

Back at their house, Sally made Maddie parade her new clothes for Lauren, as she had paid for them. She went to her room with her and helped her put on her new clothes. It wasn't until Maddie was undressing that Sally noticed her bruising. "What happened to you, Maddie?" she asked. "Who did that to you, was it your boyfriend?" Maddie was thinking how to tell her what had happened. "No, it was other men, they hurt me." "But how did they hurt you?" Sally wanted to know. "I don't remember anything, I was on drugs," she told Sally. "I don't like men, they hurt people, but not Mike, he is nice to Lauren and me," said Sally. Lauren had been privy to this conversation and thanked the Lord that all had been erased from Maddie's past. It was then that Sally showed Maddie her scarred back and buttocks. "Oh Sally, who did that?" she asked. Lauren listened with interest — would all be revealed? "I haven't told anyone but it was a brown man with slit eyes." "What did he do that for?" "Because he told me if I ever told anyone about the drugs, he would kill me. I don't want to die, so I haven't told anyone, only you, but

I am still frightened, so don't you tell anyone. We both have secrets together, they will be ours forever," said a sincere Sally. The two girls hugged each other, right here in this moment, a bond was formed that would never be broken, as they had entrusted their lives to each other. Lauren was moved, how beautiful was this? Two lonely souls had found peace together.

Mike had returned from his undercover job. He was away longer than he thought he would be, so it was going to be lovely to be with Lauren and Sally again. But now there was a third person in the house. Lauren wondered how Maddie would feel about Mike. Would she be frightened of him? She had spoken to Mike about this so they were prepared. Sally brought Maddie into the lounge to meet him. "This is Lauren's boyfriend, he is bossy like Lauren, but he is kind to her, she likes him, I do too. She even lets him sleep in her bed. He's not like the bad ones we know, Maddie. Mike, this is Maddie, my new best friend." "Nice to meet you, Maddie, I hope we can be friends?" he said. Maddie just stared, her face expressionless, but she did manage a 'Hi', then she walked back to her room.

Mike opened a bottle of wine and they both sat together and relaxed. Lauren told him about the guy coming to the fence and grabbing Maddie by the hair. "We will put an end to this in a hurry, if he ever tries it again," he told her. Sally called to Maddie to come and play swing ball with her on the front lawn. Lauren could hear laughter coming from the girls, she loved it when they were happy, but suddenly this was overshadowed by jeering. She jumped up and walked over to the window, and there standing by the fence was a group of guys taunting the girls. Maddie ran to Sally for protection, as she was frightened. Lauren opened the window and told the girls to come inside and yelled at the guys to 'bugger off'. She saw a couple of little packets lying on the grass, which had been tossed over the fence, probably by these guys. Mike wanted to deal to them, but Lauren didn't want them to know he was there, because if they returned, they wouldn't know he was there to protect them. After they disappeared he went out and picked up the packets and brought them inside. When he opened them, out fell four pills. "The bastards, they are putting temptation there for Maddie, hoping she will become hooked again. I'm worried, Lauren, I think they will be back. I will put an alert on your home tonight so if anything happens, all I have to do is ring and the police will come straight away." "Do you think they will come tonight? They wouldn't be that stupid, surely they will wait a couple of days?" asked Lauren. "Yes, you are probably right, but it will depend how many drugs are consumed, as this gives them the courage to conquer the world," replied Mike. He was right up there on this sub-ject, and he went ahead and placed an alert.

That night it all happened. The girls were in bed and Mike had just switched the light off, as he climbed in bed beside Lauren. The house was in darkness. He cuddled into Lauren and as he lay there, he thought he heard a noise. He listened, yes, there were definitely noises, not only in one place but in several, which meant there was more than one person outside the house. Mike reached for his phone and put an emergency called through to the police headquarters, asking them to come immediately to the property. If there were several guys on drugs outside, they could be dangerous, so he had to be careful and think of the girls' wellbeing, especially that of Maddie, as she would be their prime target. He told Lauren if they broke in, she was to get to Maddie and protect her, he would look after Sally. They could hear voices and there seemed to be plenty of them, so the longer they could hold off, it would give the police time to get there.

Then it all happened: glass was being smashed, the front door had been kicked in and a gang of young men had entered the house. The girls were woken by the glass smashing and they let out screams, as the house was still in darkness. Mike told Lauren to go to Maddie's room, he would make it to Sally's room before the guys came up the hallway. Suddenly there was light, someone had switched the lounge lights on, and that was when all was revelled. Six angry young guys made their way up the hallway, first to Maddie's room, where they found Maddie in Lauren's arms. The leader, Maddie's boyfriend, came straight for Lauren and punched her in the face knocking her to the ground, then he grabbed Maddie. "I told you, bitch, I would come for you." He dragged her away, after silencing her with a backhand across her face. At that very moment Mike appeared on the scene and started swinging his baton hitting two of the guys from the back, where they fell in a heap on the floor. Now he was up against four drugged-out men. The leader dragged Maddie out of the room, leaving the other guys to handle Mike. Sally rushed in, against Mike's instructions, and lashed out at the guys, when one punched her hard in the stomach, knocking her to the floor where she lay sobbing in pain. She could hear Maddie calling her, but she was helpless, she could do nothing. Lauren was also on the floor still trying to get her bearings, as she was hurt. Maddie was being dragged out through the gate and along the sand, as he was taking her in the direction of the sand dunes. She was losing consciousness; her world was collapsing once again, then darkness descended.

Mike was left to deal with the remaining three angry men. He tried to fight them but they kept coming at him. He felt panic, as he was frightened if anything happened to him, what would they do to Sally and Lauren? All he could hope for was the police to arrive soon. Suddenly the yard lit up and sirens rang out, his prayers had been answered, but what of Maddie? The police ran into the house and took charge of the guys. They thought they could take on the world, but this was short-lived. They were handcuffed and taken out to the paddy wagon. Mike lifted Lauren from the floor, her face swollen and bloodied, then he went to lift Sally up but she cried with pain. He managed to get her to a chair. Where was Maddie? She was gone. He ran in search of her, but to no avail. Lauren went to Sally and held her hand, as she was too sore to be cuddled.

Mike told the police one of the guys had got away and taken a young girl with him. Then there was a full-on search of the beach and the sand dunes for a guy and young girl. It didn't take long before they spotted a lone guy trying to make his way along the dunes, hoping not to be noticed, as he had seen the searchlights. A spotlight was shone directly upon him, then men came from all directions. He was a marked man, but there was no girl. "Where is the girl?" they asked. "What girl? I am on my own!" he shouted at them. They dragged him down from the dunes, along the beach to Lauren's house. "Is this the guy that took the girl?" they asked. Lauren told the police that was him. "Where is Maddie?" sobbed Sally. "I fixed her," and with this Mike gave him an almighty punch in the stomach sending him reeling to the floor. "If you have hurt her, you moron, you will pay dearly for this," he warned him. The police then arranged for a search to continue into the night until Maddie was found. Mike was in charge and they walked for hours searching the dunes calling her name, but there was no reply. This was cause for concern. Had he done something to her? Where was she?

Just on sunrise someone spotted a figure lying unconscious among the dunes. Mike ran to see if it was Maddie, and yes, there she lay, curled up in a little ball. He picked her up, telling her she was safe as he carried her back to Lauren's house. An ambulance was called to take her to the hospital, as no one knew what he had done to her. When the ambulance guys arrived, they also tended to Lauren and decided to take Sally with them as well, as she was in terrible pain. Lauren was heartbroken, her protection for her girls wasn't enough to save them from more pain. Then she thought, What if Mike wasn't here? Would they be here now? It could have ended a lot worse. Mike took her in his arms and she thanked him amid her tears for being here for them. "It's all over now, the girls will never be hassled again, they will be able to go onto the beach, but within sight of the house," he pointed out to Lauren. "Can you take me to the hospital? I have to be there for the girls, especially Maddie when she comes around, as she will be frightened," asked Lauren. Mike drove her to the hospital, then he left to head to the police station, as he wanted to make sure the guys were locked up so they couldn't harm anyone else. They kissed each other goodbye and Lauren thanked him once again for being there. "But you were the brave one, my little minx," he whispered to her. He felt bad when he saw her swollen face and black eye, but she was 'Lauren the Braveheart'.

Lauren was shown to the ward where both Sally and Maddie were admitted. Sally lay there sobbing, she was worried for Maddie as she was still unconscious. The nursing staff came and wheeled her bed away to the X-ray room. Although Sally was in extreme pain, all her worries had gone out to Maddie. For the little time these girls had known each other, they had formed a deep bond. They thought only they knew each other's secrets, but Lauren had overheard their confessions to each other. For this she was grateful, as now she knew it was the Asian guy who had inflicted Sally's pain. She didn't want to have to ask them separately what they had revealed to each other, as their trust would have been broken. This was all they had left, it could in no way be destroyed!

Sally's injuries included a very sore stomach and a cracked rib, which was where all the pain was coming from. The hospital wanted to keep her in overnight, but she wanted to go back to her home. Lauren talked her into staying so she would be there for Maddie, besides she had to get a new front door. It would not be glass this time, it would be made of sturdy wood, not that they would be troubled by those guys again! Mike would make sure they went down for everything in the book — all that the police could throw at them, they would go down for. Their lives were sorted!

The sun had risen and the darkness was gone. It was the beginning of a new day. Lauren had dropped off to sleep in the hospital chair while waiting on news of Maddie. Sally had been given painkillers to ease the pain caused by her cracked rib, so she was still asleep. A nurse had woken Lauren and asked her to come with her, as she wanted to talk to her in private. The examination had shown that she had not been interfered with recently, but there were old scars — did Lauren know of her past? Lauren explained that she did and that is why she took her in her care, to help her recover and return to a normal life. She had no broken bones but was hit around the head, rendering her unconscious, and there was no reason why she wouldn't make a complete recovery. "She will be a disturbed young girl for a long time, but with the proper nurturing she should come out of this okay. I can't say unscathed, because with these cases no one knows the end results. She has been through a shocking experience, one that no young girl her age should have been subjected to. She will probably never trust a man, so marriage may not be a future thought for her, but whatever happens, I hope she finds happiness somewhere, God knows she deserves it! You are doing a great job, it is a sobering thought to know there is somewhere for these girls to go, where they will be loved. I'll take you to see her as she is coming around, her mind has started to function again.

When Lauren walked into the ward, Maddie held her arms out for Lauren to hold her, as she need to feel loved. "Oh Maddie, I'm so sorry for not keeping you safe, you have been hurt again," she sobbed. "It was not your fault. The hospital told me I will never see him again, he is going away for many years. I'm glad they never hurt you too much, Lauren. Where is Sally, is she okay?" Lauren told Maddie she was in hospital with a cracked rib, and was coming home tomorrow. "Can I see her?" she asked. "I miss her." Lauren arranged with the nurse to bring Maddie back to Sally's ward so they could be together again. Tears welled up in Lauren's eyes. How appropriate for these two lost souls to be reunited again. A bond was definitely there between them and she wondered how deep it went.

A week had passed and everyone was home again in a loving happy environment. Sally was still in pain, so Maddie became her nurse. This gave Lauren more time to spend with Mike when he visited. Today he had come with some good news. The guys that had broken into the house and attacked them had every charge possible laid against them: supplying drugs, prostitution, breaking and entering, wilful damage of property, assault, obstructing the law, kidnapping, and attacking a police officer. The lightest sentence was five years and the ringleader, Maddie's boyfriend, received eight years, and when released from prison he would not be allowed to live within a 100-kilometre radius of her home. This was comforting news for Maddie; now she felt safe.

Lauren allowed the girls to walk on the beach together, but they had to stay within visual distance of the house. This way she could make sure they were safe. Most times she accompanied them, but they needed to feel independent of Lauren, so trust had to prevail. They were inseparable and Lauren noticed they were always touching and cuddling each other. Was this friendship more than just an ordinary friendship? Sally was nearly nineteen and Maddie was seventeen. Were they too young to know about feelings? Hardly — they had experienced most facets of life well before their years!

Mike arrived today with the local newspaper. There was a write-up on the front page about their ordeal. No names were mentioned, just that a local hero who had opened her home for abused girls was attacked, along with the girls, by a group of young men on drugs. The house had been broken into and wilful damage had occurred. A police officer was present on the property when this happened in the early hours of the morning, otherwise it could have ended with serious consequences. The two young girls were admitted to hospital, one unconscious and the other with a cracked rib. The hero had been punched in the face and received a black eye and swelling to her face. The offenders were known to one of the young girls. How cowardly was this? A good Samaritan who was helping young girls into rehabilitation to overcome abusive pasts was attacked by these dregs of society. What was the world coming to? Lauren asked Mike who had put this in the paper, but he didn't know. What he did say was the police station was inundated with enquiries from people as to where they could leave donations to help this local hero. The police asked for the donations be left at the Salvation Army for the 'Hero' cause, then it would be delivered to Lauren.

The following day Lauren received two lots of visitors. The first one was Anna. She had read the article in the paper and she knew straight away who the hero was. "Look at your face, Lauren, the bastards. How are the girls?" Lauren took her to the window to watch the two girls walking hand in hand along the beach. "There they go, my two girls. I'm so happy with my decision to take them in and care for them, it has been so rewarding. I love them both in their own unique ways," she told Anna. "How do you live, Lauren, you have no means of earnings?" Anna asked. "Remember the girl who the Langlands called their daughter, the one who drowned? Her parents fundraise for me so I can help these abused girls. They lost their daughter, who was their only child, and they don't want other parents to suffer every day like they do. But the sad thing is, Sally's mother doesn't care and Maddie has never mentioned anything of her past. One day I will ask her about her family, but the time hasn't been right yet. How is everything with you, Anna?"

She was hoping Lauren would not ask her this question. What was she going to tell her? She already knew the answer! "I have had a change of job also, I'm not at the Blue Water Apartments any more, Scott and I are finished. Why didn't I listen to you, Lauren? What a control freak. I can't say you didn't warn me!" "Anna, I was warned, but like you I took no notice. We have to learn by our mistakes. I will tell you something that will make you laugh. Scott would never let me into the bathroom while he was in there, it was his sacred place. After I met Mike, one day I was having a shower and Mike came in, we made love with the water cascading down our bodies, it was such fun. Fancy getting to twenty-seven and not having made love in the shower. That was the narrow-minded control freak he was, everything had to be his way and for ten years I put up with that. I feel at times I can relate on a deep personal level with Sally and Maddie." Anna laughed. She had spent less than a year with him and that was too long, he certainly had some weird ideas. "Who is his latest?" asked Lauren. "He has hired a dolly bird for his receptionist, she will be his next victim. I had to try to teach her the ropes, but she's all beauty and no brains." They both had a giggle over this.

Lauren's next visitors were the couple who had lost their daughter. They had also read the article in the paper, so came to see if Lauren and the girls were okay, as they were horrified when they read this. Here was someone kind enough to look after lost souls and this was how she was repaid! While they sat and had a cuppa with Lauren, the girls came back. Sally spoke with them and out of the blue, to everyone's surprise, she went up and hugged the lady. She knew they gave Lauren money to help them live. "Thank you, we love living with Lauren, don't we, Maddie?" She nodded in agreeance. The lady's heart was warmed, she felt for a minute her daughter had returned to her. They would continue to fundraise for Lauren and the girls, as here were two lives that were saved and they knew there would be more. The man wanted to know if he could do any repairs, but they had already been done. "We are thinking of selling our farm and moving closer to town, we will keep in touch. Keep up the good work, Lauren, look after yourself and the girls," they said as they stood up to leave. Lauren and the girls walked out and saw them off. Sally ran to the mailbox and was surprised at the number of letters that were there. "Look at all this mail, Lauren, who is writing to you?" she wanted to know. She gave them to Lauren, who was just as surprised. They went inside and opened the letters. They were full of donations and kind wishes from some of the local people who knew who their local 'hero' was!

# 12

# Preparing for the court case

The police were building a case against the Stuarts. The court case was due to begin in two weeks' time, so the more information they could put together, the stronger the case against them. The police asked Lauren to bring Sally in for an interview the next morning. When she spoke with Sally about this, she was not at all happy. "But Lauren, this is all over, I don't want to go there again, I'm a new person." "Yes, Sally, you are a new person, but those people have to be punished and put behind bars. You are the one person that can put them there," Lauren tried to explain to her. "But I don't want to remember any of that again," she said between her tears. Lauren knew these memories were unpleasant for her, or was it because she was still frightened of the threats made by the Asian guy? Were they still raw in her mind?

Was it time for Lauren to tell Sally about the young girl before her, the one that she wasn't able to rescue? If she took this all in, then she would fight for her. "Sit down, Sally, I have something I want to tell you. You know the man and lady that help us with money, do you know why they do this for us? I will tell you why. Their daughter was the Stuarts' drug mule before you. She was that drugged, one night while on her way to do a drop-off she walked into the sea and drowned. Her body was found the next day washed up on the rocks. Her body lay in the mortuary for many days; she was alone, no one knew where she was, but she was their daughter. They knew nothing of this. They miss her every single day, she never leaves their minds, that is why they fundraise for us. If I had realised sooner what was going on, I could have saved her life, but I didn't, it was too late! The Stuarts didn't care — the next day they got a new drug mule and that was you, Sally. Lives mean nothing to those people who deal and sell drugs. The money given to us by that kind couple is so I can carry on and help rescue girls like you and Maddie, to give you a loving home and a second chance at life. Their daughter didn't get that chance." "Oh Lauren, that is so sad," said Sally with tears streaming down her face. "I will help those nice people, they are helping us, so I must help them."

Maddie was sitting next to Sally and she took it all in. "Yes, Sally, good on you, you will feel hurt, we have all felt that, then you will feel better. That poor girl will smile down on you," she said in all earnest. "Do you think so, Maddie?" she asked. "Yes, because I know! When my mother died, I used to see her smiling down at me when I closed my eyes. Just because they are not here where we can see them, they are up there somewhere. But when my boyfriend started me on drugs, I lost her, she never came back. Probably because she didn't like me any more. I tried so many times to ask her to smile at me again, but she never did. Perhaps when I am good again, she might want to see me. It doesn't matter so much now that I have you and Lauren to love me." With this Sally cuddled her. Lauren was in shock. Here was Maddie talking about her life, something no one knew anything about. She was so chocked up with emotions, she couldn't hold on to them any longer. "Maddie, come here to me?" She just had to hold her and tell her how much she cared for her.

This was a new side to Maddie. She had come out of her shell, even if it was just for one moment; it spoke volumes. It was as if she believed in the afterlife, but as Lauren thought about Maddie's life, how would she have made it through if she didn't have belief? She needed something to cling to in her darkest hours. To have been used for prostitution by the lowest of lowlifes, where was her mind at in those times? Yes, she definitely must have believed in divine intervention from above!

Today was interview day at the police station. Sally, Maddie and Lauren were sitting around a desk with Mike and the head of police. "I know, Sally, this is going to be tough on you, but we must get as much information as possible on the Stuarts. As you know they are bad people," said Mike. Lauren and Mike had discussed Mr Hiroshi, but decided to leave him at the moment, best to concentrate on the Stuarts. They would deal with him later. "Could you please tell me how you met the Stuarts?" asked the chief of police. Sally told him how it all happened, that they were meant to help her get better. "What sort of drugs did you take?" She told him sometimes it was pills, other times it was powder, she didn't really know. "Did you have to pay for them?" "No, I didn't have to pay for them, they were payment for the work I did for them," she told him. Then he asked what sort of work she did. Sally told him she had to go down to the beach each night and bury the drugs in the sand, then later she had to go back and pick up the money that was buried. "Were you ever frightened?" he asked. She said she didn't really know or care, because the drugs fixed her brain, she didn't feel anything.

"Did any other people come to visit the Stuarts?" Mike looked at Lauren, he never expected this. Sally started to cry, so Maddie took her hand and told her to be brave. "A brown man with skinny eyes used to come and take a lot of money away." "Was he a nice man?" he asked, and this brought more tears from Sally. Lauren reached for her hand and squeezed it. "But if I tell you, will I die?" she sobbed. "What do you mean?" questioned the chief of police. "He told me he would kill me if I told anyone about the drugs." "No, Sally, he is locked away, he can't hurt you," he assured her. Then she proceeded to tell him how he would light a cigarette and burn her, but she wasn't allowed to cry so she just crouched in a corner and cried to herself so no one would hear her. The chief of police was shocked, he had no prior knowledge of these offences. He apologised to Sally, telling her how sad he was that this had happened. He called the meeting to a close. "Thank you, Sally, for being so brave," said Mike.

Lauren held her hand as they left the police station, as she was a little unsettled, having recalled those terrifying moments. "Am I really safe, Lauren? He told me I would die If I told anyone." "Sally, you have done the right thing. The police had to know so he can be punished, then he can't hurt anyone else. He is a dangerous man," Lauren assured her. "You are a brave person, Sally, and I love you for that," said Maddie, with great affection for her friend. As they were driving home Lauren made a suggestion: "Let's go to McDonald's." She wanted to see if Sally had put her past behind her, that she wouldn't be afraid if she saw Asian people eating there. "Yes, please, Lauren," voiced Maddie. Not a word came from Sally. They pulled into the carpark and when the girls got out, Sally took Maddie's hand and in they went. They ordered then went and sat down — they didn't have to worry about money because Lauren always paid! There was an Asian family sitting next to them, but this didn't seem to worry Sally any more. All went smoothly!

As the days were passing the girls were having less disruptions at night. Maddie still called out at times, but all it took to settle her was for Lauren to lie beside her and rub her forehead. She felt secure. Her eating habits were finally paying off, she was eating good foods and her body was starting to fill out. Her feminine body shape was coming back, also her hair was looking shiny. It wouldn't be long and they would be bra hunting, but she would have an advantage as she could try Sally's for size. She didn't have to experience the same embarrassment that Sally had.

This was a busy week. The Stuarts' trial had started so they had to be at court most mornings for when they were called upon. Lauren didn't take the girls into the courtroom, as she didn't want Sally to see them ever again. If she was needed for evidence it was to be given behind a screen. When dealing with drug syndicates, this is what witnesses demanded, to be protected. The fear was always there that there would be repercussions. This was the cold hard facts of the drug world summed up in one word: fear! Mike was a main witness, as was Lauren. Sally was to be called only if it was necessary, as the court was aware of her suffering and didn't want it to hamper her recovery. The Clarkes were in the courtroom every day; they wanted to see justice done for what happened to their daughter. The Stuarts had pleaded guilty — there was no way out for them, the evidence was stacked against them. And with the added shock that the girls were tortured unbeknown to them while they were in their presence was another black mark against them. It was a one-sided trial and 'Guilty' was the only verdict that could be reached, it was a foregone conclusion!

Mr Hiroshi was the next person to take the stand. He was still in denial in spite of all his sightings at the apartment. He knew in his own mind that the remaining girl would not speak, as he had threatened her with her life, but in the end, it came down to Sally. She could put him away for a very long time. A photo was handed to her behind the screen of Mr Hiroshi and then the sobbing started, it was heard right through the court. The judge asked her if that was the man who had hurt her. "I can't say, I'm too frightened, because he told me I would die if I said anything, so I can't say anything," she sobbed. There were gasps in the courtroom. "Does he look like the man?" asked the judge. "Yes," was all Sally could say, but that was enough. The case was over, he would be found guilty and sentenced to a long term in prison.

The trial lasted a week, it was a clear-cut case, the evidence against the Stuarts far outweighed any input by them. The bad cop Lance was dealt with through the police authorities and for his part in the receiving and distributing of drugs, he received a four-year prison sentence, plus dismissal from the police force. This was where his career ended! The Clarkes thanked Mike, Lauren and Sally for helping put their daughter's killers away, so they couldn't cause any more harm to other young girls. But sadly, this was just one drug syndicate, there were plenty more out there. It would never be the end!

# 13

# A chance to feel more grown up

Sally and Maddie ran along the beach every morning after the dishes were done. Bossy Lauren gave them jobs to do each day. Today she was going to take them to a make-up session. She wanted them to start taking care of their appearance. At the moment they were just young girls and they needed guidance to become young ladies. They were literally not girls any more, they were in their late teens, in other words, young adults. Maddie was into wearing crop-tops but poor Sally had to always wear a longer tee, so as to hide her scars; they were with her for life, they would never go away. Every morning Sally lay on the grass while Maddie massaged cream onto her back, trying to remove them, but it never happened. This affected her personally, but Maddie assured her it was no big deal, they didn't worry her. She knew the story behind them, and they were part and parcel of Sally.

Lauren had arranged with a beauty parlour to have one-on-one tuition with the girls. She thought it would be good for them to learn how to apply make-up and with this gain a little confidence. It was time they experienced what it was like to act a little grown up. The ladies were very good showing the girls the different skin types and what suited each girl. As the make-up was applied the changes were amazing, their faces glowed and came alive. It was amazing what a difference a little colour made! "This is exciting, Lauren," said Maddie. The girls were loving it. She told them to pick six products each to take home and practise with. "Thank you, Lauren, that was so neat," they both echoed. Tomorrow it was the hairdresser.

The girls' hair was looking healthy now, so it was time for them to have it styled. Lauren bought them a hairstyle magazine so they could have a look through and decide what cut they wanted. They sat together and picked out styles for each other, not for themselves. Lauren was noticing they were making decisions for each other, not independently, also they were touching and cuddling a lot. She did wonder if this was a girl thing, or if it was a deeper affection. This wasn't the first time she had thought along these lines!

As Lauren was organising tea, the phone rang. "Hello, Lauren, this is Di Clarke." Who was this? she wondered, as she tried to put a face to this name. Then it clicked, this was the mother of the drowned girl. "We have sold our farm and move out in a fortnight. We were wondering if the girls would like to come and spend a weekend with us in the country." Lauren was surprised. The girls had never been away from her or each other. How would they feel about this? Then as she thought about it, she decided this would be a good opportunity to separate Sally and Maddie, to see how they would function without each other. "Hi, Di, how would you feel about having just Sally? Maddie is not quite ready yet." "Yes, that would be lovely. We will pick her up on Friday and bring her back on Sunday, when we come to church," said a happy Mrs Clarke. Lauren wondered how the girls were going to react to this separation. She would keep it to herself until nearer the end of the week.

Today was their hair appointment, and they were excited and frightened at the same time. No one had touched their hair, so this was another new experience. Lauren was gradually introducing them into the real world again. It was time. Sally was first in the chair. It was hard for her to sit still, especially when she was nervous. She let Maddie tell the hairdresser what she wanted. They had spent most of the night trying to sort out what they thought they wanted. Now that they were here, decisions were changing. The hairdresser said what she thought would suit their personalities, so again it changed. Two hours later emerged two new-look girls, both unable to stop looking at the other. They were amazed at how different they looked, just by getting their hair styled. Lauren was pleasantly surprised. They looked grown up and she wondered if they would feel more mature. She took the girls to a nice restaurant for lunch and they couldn't take their eyes off each other. This was a different look for them both, and they still hadn't got used to it. It brought about a lot of giggles.

When they arrived home, they went straight to Maddie's room and began to experiment with their make-up. Lauren heard a lot of laughter coming from the bedroom and wondered what they would look like when they emerged. Once again, she was pleasantly surprised. They had applied the make-up as they were shown, so it proved to Lauren they were taking things in, they were engaging their brains. They had to learn that life was not all play, there had to be serious decisions made at times. One was coming up: they were going to be separated for a weekend. How were they going to accept this?

Thursday had arrived and the girls were at the beach when Mike came to visit Lauren. They hadn't seen much of each other lately and they were missing their time together. He was ready to settle down with Lauren and the girls, he loved that she cared for them. She was talking of filling the last room with a new needy girl. The hospital had rung to say they had a young girl who desperately needed one-on-one attention, would Lauren come and visit her to see if she would like to care for her. She hadn't told the girls as yet. Now would be the time to go and see her, if Mike would stay and be there for the girls. He was happy to do this so Lauren went and changed and drove to the hospital. She was met by the nurse who had rung her, the one she was familiar with, so she explained everything she knew about Hannah's background — well, the little she knew of it! She walked with Lauren down the corridor to the gated unit. The door was unlocked and locked again when they went through.

There lay a young girl who was restrained in the bed, just as she remembered Sally not so long ago. She was devoid of expression, but this was not unusual for drug addicts. The nurse left Lauren with her, to see if she thought she could help this poor soul. Lauren sat on her bed and reached for her hand, but it was clenched. She held on to it but nothing happened, she couldn't feel any connection with this girl. Then as she went to take her hand away, her fist unclenched and she held on to Lauren's hand. Her heart melted. How could she walk away and leave this child? There was a little hope there, she needed to be loved. Yes, this was going to be her next charge.

When Lauren returned home the girls were sitting talking to Mike. "Where have you been, Lauren?" asked Sally, but this was typical of her, one expected to be questioned. "Just out," was Lauren's reply. "You didn't tell me the girls had their hair done, they look so different, so grown up," said Mike. Of course, this made them feel important. "Wait until you see us with make-up on," replied Sally and they ran to their bedrooms. Now that the coast was clear, Mike asked Lauren about the new recruit. She told him how it all went, she couldn't walk away from her, she had to be there for her. Just listening to Lauren was enough for Mike to know that this was going to be a happening thing. "She is lost to this world, but I can't leave her there, Mike, she must come home to us, we can only but try!"

Lauren continued: "I haven't told the girls yet, but they are going to be separated this weekend. The Clarkes asked for them both to go and spend the weekend with them on their farm, but I am a little concerned, so Sally is going on her own. I don't know how they will take this as they have never been separated. I'm sure there will be a protest, but I'm not going to give in. You know, Mike, I think their friendship is deeper than that. I have noticed little things that tell me they have deep feelings for each other. I am worried!" "Would that be so wrong, Lauren, with what has happened to them? We know Maddie can never have children, so if they can make each other happy, then so be it. This does happen in the real world. Neither likes men and who can blame them, so if they can make each other happy, just accept it," said an understanding Mike. Lauren loved that Mike saw things for what they really were. He had seen the horrid things that these girls had endured, so

he could understand why they could never have a relationship with a man.

"What do you think, Mike?" asked Sally as they came
back into the lounge all made up. "If I wasn't engaged to
Lauren, I might have been swayed by you two girls," he
answered. "Yuk!" was Sally's answer. Maddie just stood
and smiled, she was the gentle one. Even if she thought the
same as Sally, she would never say it. "I must admit you
both look so grown up, not like young girls any more, more
like young ladies." This made them feel proud. Lauren
hoped they would act a little less girlish and more towards
a young adult! Perhaps when Hannah arrived, things
would be different? She would set them tasks to do, to
make them more responsible. But her thoughts drifted
back to tomorrow, when Sally was going to be picked up
by the Clarkes and taken away. She still didn't know about
this. Lauren would wait until Mike was gone, in case she
threw a tantrum. This she was expecting!

After the dishes were cleared up, and Mike had left,
Lauren asked the girls to come and sit by her. She decided
to break the news about their new guest that was coming.
Hopefully this was going to soften the blow for what was
about to follow. "Her name is Hannah, she is very sick, just
like you girls were, she needs to be loved and cared for.
She will be in hospital for another week at least. After the
weekend we will go and visit her together. How do you feel
about us having someone else to look after?" she asked.
The girls looked at each other. Did they want to have to
share Lauren with another? This needed thinking about.
"Now I have something else to tell you. Tomorrow, Sally,
the Clarkes are going to pick you up and take you out
to their farm for the weekend." "Is Maddie coming?" was
the first question from Sally. "No, you are going on your

own." "But I can't leave Maddie, we are good friends, we love each other," she said. Lauren wondered in what context she meant this. She answered, "Yes, we all love each other here. It will only be for two nights, Sally, then you will be back." Maddie sat very quietly. Sally was doing all the talking, but they were her feelings exactly. "No, I can't go, Lauren, not without Maddie," she sobbed. "I'm sorry but you are going, Sally. I promised them and when I make a promise, I always keep it. You know that. They lost their only child to drugs, she was the girl I was too late to save. Please, Sally, they need you to go. They have sold their farm and are moving to town. They just want you there." Lauren didn't think things would get this bad. How close was the bond between Sally and Maddie?

At mid-afternoon on Friday, the Clarkes arrived to collect Sally. Lauren had told her she must appear grateful for her weekend away, not to be grumpy, that she would be annoyed if Sally let her down. "All right, bossy Lauren, but never do this again," she warned. The two girls clung to each other and shed tears, it was as if two lovers were being parted! Maddie was very quiet and as the Clarkes drove away, she ran into the house and flopped on her bed in tears. Lauren felt sad for what she had done and now she could see that there was a deep connection between the girls. She left Maddie to settle down. Two hours later she had not come out of her room, so Lauren knocked on her door. It was open but she never entered without being asked in. She went and lay on Maddie's bed beside her and put her arms around her. "What is wrong, Maddie, why are you sad?" she asked. "I don't want Sally to go away without me." "But it is only for two nights, then she will be back." "But two nights is a long time, Lauren. Sally and I love each other, one day we are going to live together," she told her. This completely threw Lauren. Had they discussed their future, was this her thoughts playing out? "But you are both young, you might meet other people?" "If you mean men, the answer is no, we have discussed this. Neither of us trusts men, we don't like them, and you know why, Lauren." This she could understand. Would it be so wrong for Sally and Maddie to live together and be happy? Then Lauren began to wonder if she had done wrong by the girls, had she let this relationship grow without trying to stop it happening? Did the blame lie with her?

Maddie moped around all weekend. Lauren went for walks along the beach with her, hoping she would forget Sally for a while, but she still looked sad. They played ball together but the usual laughter didn't ring out, it was a subdued atmosphere. Lauren had to admit she missed Sally's outspoken ways, she had become so attached to these two girls. Perhaps by bringing a new girl into the home would take some of the focus off Sally and Maddie. "Lauren, what time is Sally going to be back today, I hope I don't have to wait too long?" asked Maddie. "No, it should be soon, as the Clarkes are coming in to church this morning." With this she walked out to the gate and patiently waited for her friend to come home. Lauren watched her from the window; it was sad to see the upset she had caused Maddie. If she had known it was going to be this hard for them to be parted, she would have changed her decision. Then the car arrived and Maddie ran onto the pavement waiting for Sally to get out. They embraced each other with a mixture of tears and joy. Sally thanked the Clarkes and took Maddie's hand and they ran into the house together.

Lauren was afraid to ask how the weekend went. She was frightened that Sally might have been a pain, but she had to know. "How was Sally, did she behave herself?" she asked. "We loved having her, Lauren, she is so funny and brought happiness to our home, something that has been missing for a long while. There were moments when we thought we had Kirsty back. My God, she must have suffered, I noticed the scars on her back when she bent over. I can't help wondering if he did the same to Kirsty. Do you know, Lauren? I cried when I thought about it." How could Lauren tell her the truth, that in fact it had happened to her daughter? They had suffered enough without any more setbacks, so she decided to let this secret stay buried along with Kirsty. "That is so sad, no wonder these girls are damaged mentally. You are doing a wonderful job, Lauren! We have discussed what we want to do with the money from our farm. We hope to buy a small ownership flat in town, then the rest of the money we want to put in trust, for you and the girls. You must be able to carry on, it is important that someone looks after them. It all costs money and we have no one to leave our money to. Kirsty would be happy to know we have done this, it will be with her blessing," said a grateful Mrs Clarke. Lauren hugged her and thanked her from the bottom of her heart. The Clarkes then left to go to church.

There were times when she did wonder if she might have to get a job, to keep her home going. That was until she received a visit from the Salvation Army who had brought money for Lauren, this being the donations for the 'Hero' fund. Up until this date the public had donated $40,000 and each day the money was still coming in. The officer told Lauren that people were outraged to hear what had happened to a good Samaritan who was there to help the community. They were happy to know that the young lads were now serving a prison sentence and were off the streets.

The house was happy and alive again now that Sally was home. She told Lauren and Maddie she had a nice weekend, the Clarkes were friendly people, she even slept in Kirsty's room. It was lovely as all her treasures were still there. "Mrs Clarke said she was going to put everything of Kirsty's in a big box and bring them to our house for us girls, so I said yes please!" I bet you did, thought Lauren to herself. The girls spent most of the afternoon together. Lauren took particular notice of their displays of affection for each other and it definitely went deeper than just a friendship! She decided she would make an appointment with a psychologist to have a talk and find out if this was normal in this situation.

That night the girls went to bed early. Lauren could hear a lot of laughter coming from their rooms. It was lovely to have this happy vibe back again. Lauren decided to do the same and have an early night, perhaps curl up with a book. There wasn't much reading done before she dropped off to sleep. When she woke in the morning, she felt uncomfortable, no wonder as she had gone to sleep lying on her book. She dressed and as she passed Sally's room, she noticed she wasn't in her bed, which she thought was strange. Perhaps she was getting something to eat, but no, she wasn't in the kitchen. Lauren came back to check on Maddie and there lying in the bed cuddled together were the two girls. Lauren was shocked, she didn't know how to handle this. Would she tell them it wasn't acceptable? She just stood there, unable to take in what she was confronted with. Suddenly Sally stirred and saw Lauren standing there. "It's all right, Lauren, we love each other. You let Mike sleep in your bed because you love him." "But Sally, we are grown-ups and we are girlfriend and boyfriend," she fired back. "We will never have boyfriends, Lauren, we have talked about it, you should know why!" This hit Lauren hard, yes, she could understand why, but was this right? "Get dressed and come out and we will talk about it."

When the girls arrived for breakfast, they came hand in hand. "Before you say anything, bossy Lauren, I will be first. Maddie and I have talked about this for ages. We have so much fun together, we are happy and we love each other. When you made us part for that weekend, I cried all night wondering if Maddie was missing me. She needs me. I am the strong one. She needs a strong person to protect her, she couldn't protect herself because she is soft and quiet, you know that," stated Sally. Tears came to Lauren's eyes. What could she say? What Sally had said was all true: Maddie relied on Sally, she was her strong half. "Because this is not a normal relationship, it frightens me. You are both still young, do you really know what you want?" she asked. "But Lauren, we are not normal girls, we haven't had a normal life, look at me, I am scarred for life but Maddie doesn't mind, she knows what happened. I won't let anyone else see me. We don't like men, they hurt us. We love each other, please be happy for us?" she pleaded. Lauren was stunned. Was this really Sally talking? She seemed so grown-up. "Please, Lauren!" begged Maddie. Lauren burst into tears. She took the girls in her arms. How could things be any different? They had been to hell and back and now they had found happiness in each other. Didn't they deserve that? she asked herself ... The answer came back as yes!

# 14

# Guest number three

The girls and Lauren were on their way to the hospital to see Hannah. They were excited, a new girl would be coming to live with them soon. When they arrived, a nurse took them down the corridor to the gated unit, which she unlocked to let them through. There, sitting on the bed, was Hannah. Lauren had sat with her a few days ago but she was not at all well, so she didn't know if she would remember her. "Hello, Hannah, I have brought my girls to meet you. This is Sally and Maddie. They have been sick just like you, but they are better now." "Hi, Hannah!" Sally greeted her. She looked at the girls and smiled, then she turned to Lauren. "Why didn't you come back? I was waiting for you to hold my hand, I needed you." Then she burst into tears. "I'm sorry, Hannah, but I had to go to court. I will never leave you again. We will come and visit you each day, then when you are released from hospital, we will take you home with us, won't we, girls?" "Yes, we will have fun, we are funny, I think, aren't we, Lauren?" asked Sally. How could Lauren not agree! She was happy she had brought the girls. As they chatted away to Hannah, she seemed to relate better to someone her own age. "Gosh, you are thin." Maddie had spoken. "You looked the same when I first saw you, Maddie, but look at you now. That is what eating healthy does, it builds you up. You will fill out like Maddie when you start eating again, Hannah. It will take a little while, but it will happen!" An hour had passed and a nurse came in with some pills for her to take. She explained these were to help Hannah with the 'lows' she was experiencing and to help remove the toxins from her body. The pills would make her sleepy, so they decided it was time to go, so she could get the rest she needed to get better. "We will see you tomorrow, Hannah," said Sally. Maddie smiled at her and waved goodbye. Lauren took her hand and told her she would care for her, then she felt a little squeeze as her eyes closed.

This morning Mike had a couple of hours off so he came to visit. Lauren wanted to go and speak to a psychologist about the girls, so asked if he would mind waiting with the girls until she came back. She explained what had happened with Sally and Maddie, but Mike didn't see it as a big deal, he had already said it was understandable in their circumstances. But Lauren just wanted to be reassured! She drove to town and met with a professional, who she felt would help her overcome her anxiety about the situation. She explained the girls' lives and now they had become more than just friends. "Understandably so, to think they have found happiness after all they have been through is remarkable. Let them have the happiness they deserve. Even if they hadn't met each other, they would have found another female partner elsewhere. There was never going to be a male in either of their lives, the trust had been taken from them. Don't fret over this, it is perfectly understandable! To try to separate them would do more harm than good, as they would feel society had abandoned them." Lauren thanked the lady and left her office feeling a lot more comfortable with the situation.

When Lauren arrived home, guess who wanted to know where she had been? "You didn't tell us you were going somewhere?" questioned Sally. "I didn't know myself until I got there." Sally stood and thought about this, then shook her head and walked off. Mike wanted to talk to Lauren about their life. Now that the court case was over and all the bad people were dealt to, it was time for them to start making some arrangements for their future together. "I don't want a big wedding, Mike, just something cosy and nice on the beach, with a few close friends and of course I will have Sally and Maddie as my bridesmaids." "Of course!" agreed Mike. They agreed to work on their future plans over the next few months.

Today Hannah was being released from the hospital and everyone was excited. But before they went, Lauren called a meeting. "Girls, I have made a decision, a big decision. Before we go to pick Hannah up, you have a job to do." "What now, Lauren?" asked Sally. "You can move your beds into one room and be together. This will be our secret, so off you go and do it right now. Then Hannah will have a choice of rooms." Sally just stood and looked at Lauren, but Maddie ran to her and thanked her. "You surprise me, Lauren, but we both love you dearly," and away they ran. There was no deciding which room it was to be. It had to be the yellow room where the sun shone all the time! Once the excitement had died down over the shifting in together, and the beds were in their rightful places, it was time to go to the hospital.

Hannah was waiting in the hospital foyer for Lauren

and the girls to arrive. She was feeling a little excited. Anything would be better than being behind locked doors in the hospital! She had packed her bag, someone had dropped off her clothing so she wasn't coming empty-handed. She liked the girls and Lauren seemed a caring person. She was wondering where she was going to live. Would she have to share a room? But soon she would find out. As Lauren pulled up outside the entrance, the girls climbed out and went to greet Hannah. Lauren had a meeting with the duty nurse about Hannah's medication, and any other problems that accompanied her. The medication had to be administered at certain times, so this was all listed for her. She had to have a sleep after lunch each day for the next fortnight for the medication to work, to help keep her moods in check. Once all this was noted it was time to head home. Sally and Maddie were in the back seat so Hannah could sit in the front with Lauren. It was a silent journey home, but when they pulled up by the sea, Hannah came alive. "I love the beach and the sand, is this where I am going to live?" she asked. "Yes, this is your home until you get better," answered Lauren. She climbed out of the car and ran to the beach. "I love it here already," she yelled. The girls got out and joined her and they all held hands and ran along the sand. Lauren felt tears welling up in her eyes. How lovely, now she had three girls!

The Clarkes had bought a modern apartment and had moved into town. They had made an appointment with their solicitor and asked Lauren to come along, as they wanted her to sign some papers. When it was revealed that their farm had sold for $8,000,000, they wanted to put $6,000,000 in a trust for Lauren and her home for lost girls. They suggested she buy the adjacent section and build a new home that would house more girls. Lauren was in shock — so much money! How kind were these people? She couldn't hide her tears of joy. Now she could look after more needy girls. She knew Sally and Maddie would be with her forever, she was their mentor, their mother, their everything, really! They would be good helpers as they understood and had experienced life in its darkest hours. Mrs Clarke asked Lauren if she could come and teach the girls how to cook and bake, then they could sell their produce to raise funds. This arrangement would suit everyone. Lauren went to the Clarkes and hugged them and thanked them for their kindness. As she got into her car she sat and thought back over her life, how she had changed. She had started her working life happy, then a dark cloud descended when she made a wrong choice that lasted ten years. Once that cycle had been broken, a new life emerged. It didn't matter the degree of suffering, but to suffer in itself was enough to understand what others had endured!

Hannah was fitting in well with the girls. Her suffering didn't go as deep as Sally and Maddie's, as she had been introduced to drugs in the restaurant trade where she was working. She didn't suffer sexual abuse or torture, so her convalescing was solely to beat her drug addiction. When Lauren treated the girls to a lunch out, Hannah was the first to remark if she saw a cute guy. Sally retaliated with a 'Yuk' and Maddie remained silent. This was a different outlook for Hannah!

# 15

# Lauren's dreams are materialised

The wedding day had finally arrived. After many set dates that never materialised, today's date had survived. Lauren just wanted a quiet wedding on the beach, by her home. Mrs Clarke, Anna and the girls had all the catering under control. Mr Clarke had to be torn away from his gardening, as he was setting out the grounds for Lauren's 'Lost Souls' home. The contractors were nearly finished, so he wanted to have everything ready for the opening in a fortnight. Lauren wanted to get married before the home opened, as once more girls arrived, she wouldn't have time to think about wedding plans. Sally and Maddie were the bridesmaids and they were so excited. Lauren had matching dresses made of pale-yellow lace for them, as she never forgot Sally's words: 'I like yellow, it's warm like the sun. That would mean the sun would shine all the time'. That was what she wanted her life to be like. Lauren wore a white satin and lace wedding dress with a lovely floppy straw hat. She looked relaxed and happy. Mr Clarke walked her up to her groom, it was as if he was giving his lost daughter away. He felt this was a great privilege, and Lauren felt he hadn't been robbed of a duty that was rightfully his.

The celebrant performed the wedding and Lauren and Mike said their vows and exchanged rings. Now they were husband and wife. The police formed a guard of honour, which the happy couple walked through and then they all took a walk along the beach. The breakfast had been set up under a marquee so everyone found their seat and settled. The police superintendent stood up and gave a speech, telling all how brave Lauren had been in the initial stages of putting away a drug syndicate. Her alertness to what was happening around her had set the ball rolling. "As for Mike, he is one of our most dedicated drug squad members, he has a job to do and that is exactly what he does. His concern for the young vulnerable kids today exceeds his duty, and this is why this is a match made in heaven. Together, Mike and Lauren will give many young girls a second chance at life. They are to be admired and we will support them whenever we can. Cheers to this special couple!"

The next people to speak were Mr and Mrs Clarke. They told the guests how they became involved with Lauren. And that they looked on Sally as their own daughter. Because they still suffer each day with their loss, they didn't want other parents to have to go through the same. But today their suffering had come to an end. "I feel I am the luckiest man alive, today I have walked my friend Lauren down the aisle. This was a parental duty I thought I was robbed of. I am so happy, thank you, Lauren, you have made me a very happy man." As Lauren looked around the room, there wasn't a dry eye anywhere.

Now it was on to the food, everyone was hungry. Well, Sally and Maddie were; this was all over their head, they couldn't understand why a woman wanted a man. Lauren was so happy, she was ready to settle with the man she loved dearly. Their lives had been busy, but tonight they would be able to go to bed together and wake up in each other's arms. This was a pattern that would carry on forever ... They had a ready-made family before they even married. This subject had come up for discussion and by mutual agreement they decided not to have children of their own. They loved their girls and there would be many more to care for. Why bring more children into the world when there were girls already here to care for?

Lauren's wedding day was perfect, it was everything she could have wished for. Once all the guests had gone, apart from Mr and Mrs Clarke and the girls, she sat down and put her feet up. These were the special people in her life so she had asked them to stay behind so they could all have a quiet drink together. Mike took the top off a bottle of bubbly and poured everyone a drink including the girls. Little did she know that Mike had arranged for the Clarkes to stay overnight so he could whip Lauren off to a nice resort for their wedding night. The limousine would be there shortly, everyone knew including the girls. Sally had packed a little overnight bag for Lauren with her toothbrush and toothpaste and she had put in a lovely nightie she had found in her drawer. She thought it would be nice for her to it put on before she climbed into bed. She had even put a book in, in case Lauren wanted to read before she went to sleep, as she did most nights. But tonight, there would be no reading, but then Sally wouldn't understand what went on between a man and a woman on their wedding night. Suddenly there was great excitement as the limo pulled up at the gate. Lauren had no idea what was happening. Sally handed her the bag and Mike whipped her off her feet and carried her to the waiting vehicle.

Lauren was still wondering what was happening as they were being driven up the street. "Where are we going, Mike?" she asked. "It is our wedding night, we are spending it somewhere special. I have booked a honeymoon suite where we will have no interruptions, no nosy girls asking what we are doing or when are we getting up. That will start soon enough," he laughed. Lauren was happy that they were on their own. All hell could break loose tonight and no questions would be asked. Mike told her Sally had packed her bag, so this was going to be a surprise. Had she thought logically, or not thought at all? Soon all would be revealed.

As they entered the honeymoon suite Lauren's eyes nearly popped out of her head. It was beautiful and there on the bench was a platter with fruit, cheeses and biscuits along with a bottle of champagne. "This is lovely, Mike, you are such a thoughtful guy, that's why I love you. Just think what brought us together. If that drug syndicate had not occupied that apartment then neither of us would be standing here today and I would never have saved Sally or found Maddie. It makes me sad to think I might not have saved those girls from the seedy underworld." "This is our wedding night and we are here, so let's enjoy ourselves. You are an angel sent to me, Lauren, and for that I love you dearly. You have such compassion, such love, that you share with everyone, but tonight you will only share it with me. Tonight, you are mine," he said lovingly. Lauren decided to unpack the bag that Sally had given her. The first thing out was the toothbrush, then the toothpaste, next came the book, and last of all was the nightie. "Just leave that in there, we don't need that tonight," he joked. "But Sally will be upset if I didn't wear my nightie to bed, that would be so wrong, especially when I am sleeping with a man," said Lauren with a cheeky smile. "Come here, my little minx, we will shock her tonight ...

Today was the grand opening of Lauren's 'Lost Souls' home. It had taken eighteen months to build and set the grounds out. Mr Clarke had worked relentlessly on the grounds, they were his pride and joy. The Salvation Army band were in full swing welcoming all the people who wanted to be here today. It was not by invite, it was an open affair, open to all those families who had lost sons and daughters to the underworld of drugs. The building was on display to let the public see that this rehabilitation centre was here for young girls who needed help. A lot of money had come from public donations, so this was one way of saying thank you. The police department were also heavily involved, as Lauren was their 'hero'. Mrs Clarke, Sally, Maddie and Hannah had baked all week to cater for this special occasion. Once the crowd had gathered it was Lauren's big moment. "I am proud to be standing here today, my dream has been realised. From deep down in my heart, my first big thank you goes to Mr and Mrs Clarke, who donated generously so I was able to buy this piece of land and build my rehabilitation centre, and to the public who kindly gave donations, to you all I am truly grateful. This is all for a necessary cause, one that resides deep in my heart. I have brought three young girls back from the brink of darkness and given them a second chance at life. They have become my daughters. Please come here and stand beside me, Sally, Maddie and Hannah. They are living proof that if nurtured and loved there is a life after drugs. This problem is growing with each day that passes, so we must try to save these young girls who are vulnerable. From next week we have six new girls coming to live with us, who at this moment lie restrained in hospital beds overcoming withdrawal symptoms that cause seizures and other terrible side effects. It is sad to see what these girls go through in their first few weeks. But we will be here to love and care for them and bring renewed hope into their lives. But today you are here to enjoy this new facility, so please stop by the kitchen and have a cuppa and a bite to eat. Last but not least I would like to say a huge thank you to my husband, Mike. He has been my main support, he loves our girls and is fighting relentlessly to remove drug dealers from our society. Please feel free to talk to me at any time. Thank you all." A roar went up from the crowd.

Several months on, sadly Mr Clarke passed away. This meant the home became Mrs Clarke's lifeline. Sally and Maddie had shifted into their new flat together, which was built specially for them, separate from the main home but on the same grounds. This left Lauren and Mike with their house to themselves. They both needed this privacy. Mrs Clarke spent most of her time teaching the girls basic culinary skills. She loved all the girls, but Sally was special to her. She had survived when her daughter Kirsty had not, so she was thought of as a substitute daughter and they formed a close bond. Hannah was now in a relationship with a young man and was working in the kitchen at the hospital. Now that she was fully recovered, she had moved out of the home so someone else could get the love and care they needed to start on their journey to recovery. The home had ten rooms and they were all full. Sally and

Maddie had set patients they had to care for, so they were separated for a big part of the day. This was good for Maddie as it helped her to grow in confidence, and she had to make her own decisions. This did not interfere with how they felt about each other; they were still inseparable. Lauren could see now that things would never change. They belonged together and she was so proud of them and what they had achieved.

Lauren found the workload at the home very intense, as ten girls all in different stages of rehabilitation put a lot of stress on her, especially at night. She needed someone else full time to work alternate night shifts, to help spread the workload. Sally and Maddie were fine with the day work, but the night shift was a big responsibility, as this was when the girls were at their most vulnerable. Lauren approached Anna to see if she would be willing to take on a full-time position at the home. She was thrilled. This would be a change from reception work. She had been through a lot with Lauren and understood how the girls had suffered. They had worked together before and had a good rapport. They had even shared the same man, with both relationships ending in disaster! Who next, Scott?

Each Sunday was open day at the 'Lost Souls' home. As the girls recovered, they spent time in the kitchen learning to cook and bake. A stall was set up in the grounds and this was where their culinary delights were sold as a fundraiser. It also taught the girls the responsibility of handling money. Sally's favourite saying, 'Lauren will pay', had long gone, as now they were paid a wage which they had to budget and live on. Sally and Maddie had taken a long time to truly understand the workings of the real world, but they were Lauren's first girls so they were spoilt a little, but then they had suffered more than most! The new girls had to learn a lot quicker as now there was a waiting list for girls to come to Lauren's home. It was a wonderful asset to the area and a much needed one.

Lauren was disappointed she couldn't save all the girls. Several had slipped through the cracks but they were never going to be saved. She couldn't offer them any more than her best, but sometimes this was not enough. For these girls there was no light ahead, so they descended into a life of darkness, fuelled by drugs. This she was very sad about, but she had to let go, she wasn't God, she couldn't save the world ... but then neither could he!

Mike was with Lauren all the way. Her calling was to save the young girls and his was to punish the offenders, to take them out of public places, or anywhere for that matter and try to make the world a safer place for the young people. "But in reality, Lauren, the drug scene will survive, there is too much quick money to be made. It only takes one little pill or a dab of powder to pass from a dealer to a user and someone makes money. How easy is that? How horrible is that? But these are the cold hard facts and it is young innocent kids who suffer. The temptations are out there for our young people today. There will always be the vulnerable who are preyed upon, or the experimental kids who will give anything a go, but in the end, with the same result, a life of drugs and darkness, bringing with it heartache for loved ones, and sometimes division of families. These are the shocking truths, it is a sad world out there," said Mike, speaking with a heavy heart.

Mike and his drug squad see this as a plague, a 'widespread infestation'. As the modern drugs become more lethal, the consequences suffered will grow beyond belief. A great money-spinner for some brings tragedy to others.

For drug dealers, money comes before mercy, such is life in their murky underworld.

'It is almost at boiling point now!'

A pill for a life ... what a trade! How tragic has life become for the vulnerable young of today?

# About the author

Margaret Nyhon lives in Alexandra, in the Central Otago province of New Zealand, where she writes, paints and practises the crafts of printing and bookbinding. She has worked extensively in hospitality management in New Zealand and resort management in Australia. The urge to trace her family history led her to the writing of her first non-fiction work, *de Marisco*. She has since written several fiction and non-fiction works. Margaret is married and has three adult children and two grandsons.

# Other titles by the author

## Non-fiction

de Marisco
Freedom Knows No Boundaries
A Wake-up Call
A Shattered Dream Across the Tasman

## Fiction

Isobella (Book 1 in the *Isobella* series)
Isobella: Self Redemption (Book 2 in the *Isobella* series)
Papa's Girl Emmeline
Betrayal by an Irish Rose
Revenge for an English Lord (sequel to *Betrayal by an Irish Rose*)
For Girls' Eyes Only

## Coming Soon

Pimchan's Journey Away From Poverty
*Based on a true story*